Prophecy Trilogy: New Moon

LIZ BULLARD

Liz Bullard Writes
Since 2021

Liz Bullard Writes

To my family, both by blood and by heart, who have shaped and supported me throughout my life, and to the ones who have become a part of my journey over time. This book is dedicated to the bonds we have formed, the memories we have shared, and the love that binds us all together.

Contents

CHAPTER ONE

1

The blood-soaked earth groans for peace, and the ground shakes from warriors immersed in battle. The land, usually painted with the smell of coastal air and lavender fields, is covered with the haze of smoke as fire elementals set fields ablaze, burning the opposing side. To the sky are two suns. One that rises and falls signaling day, another that burns red like the blood of the fields. It is the Crimson Sun that signals an epic battle more fierce than this will soon begin.

Beating war drums and battle cries reminds warriors and villagers of failed peace talks between the Elders of Zodia and the Ox Nation. After months of keeping Ox Nation to the fields, the front lines are now visible from the Elders' perch. Their villa, a sanctuary built inside a towering oak tree, cast their gaze far and wide. Their dwelling place holds the four who make up the council of Elders and their ruling sage, Onmai.

Protected from the front lines, the Elders debate strategy and safety as Onmai's wise eyes assess the casualties lost and projected lives yet to lose.

An Elder, tall and weary, conceals the shadows under his eyes with his darkened veil, speaks, "Debating is futile. We hear the war drums. Leaving is our utmost priority."

"We have more warriors to send. We will not abandon our home," cries a frail Elder hunched on his cane.

"If we are to move those in the village safely, we will need those warriors," speaks a woman no older than the veil-wearing Elder.

"Where would we go, Navi? Ox Nation seeks to take control of all our lands. Do you think they will not hunt us?" snips a pixie-looking woman edging closer to Navi.

"If you are so ready to defend our land, Aster, run down to the front lines. Our warriors' lives are blown away as easily as a flame in a windstorm. Our options are few," Navi shoots back.

The two women are upon each other enough to feel the heat leave their bodies.

"Enough, Navi is right. Our warriors are dying, which means we are losing. Ox Nation is far more ruthless and boarish. Slipping away now will save our people. We can repopulate and rebuild from the youth and childbearing that remain."

"Do you hear yourself, Gaia," sneers the frail Elder hobbling closer. "We will not repopulate our people like they are cattle."

"What is the matter, Fin? Afraid you won't be used for that task?" Gaia sneers.

The four Elders' voices raise, their noise, like the war drums, clouds Onmai's thoughts. Shifting her focus from the maps and reports to that of the feuding counsel, she speaks in a tone that silences the room.

"Quiet. I will not have war within my counsel and on the fields."

Murmured apologies leave the Elders' lips as they turn their attention to the maps and strategies. They discuss reports presented by the generals on the field, searching for paths and finding no answers.

Sage Onmai runs her hands over her skin, a shade of brown reminiscent of the afterglow of a dawn sky. Her fingers press down on her cheekbones, smoothening her deepening wrinkles and throbbing bones.

"Elder Onmai!" roars a scout, seeking her attention.

"Here, child. Speak. What is the condition on the battlefield?"

Onmai moves from the maps, meeting the breathless scout. The scout, a little one no more than twelve and no taller than her waist, tries to regain his breath.

"The battle continues. Our troops push back the Ox Nation, but their warriors are many. The generals urge for more assistance. They do not know how long they can keep up this fight."

"We should take this opportunity to move who we can from our dwelling," says Elder Gaia. His counterparts agree, shifting their speech to talk of departure.

"No," Onmai snarls. "I will not leave our home or our warriors. I have faith they will be victorious."

"Faith does nothing for the dead, and dead is what we'll be if we stay. Ox Nation has far less to lose than us," says Navi.

The Elders, even those who once supported staying in the fight, encourage fleeing. Yet Onmai does not waver.

"I will stop no one who wishes to depart our home. But know this: I will not welcome any deserter back into our ranks. I will cast you out like a dog who has bitten its master. Am I clear?"

The whispers cease. The Elders are motionless amidst the smoky scent of the fire and the ringing of metal clashing, waiting for their next order. Taking their silence as obedience, Onmai turns her attention to the scout.

"Young one, you have done well, and I know your legs are weary. But I have a selfish request to ask of you."

The young one edges closer, intent on hearing her request.

Placing a gentle hand on his shoulder, she continues, "I need to know if two warriors are still in the battle. I need you to search for news on Eli and Talia. My heart burns for all my warriors, but these two are special to me. Do you know of them?"

The young scout nods, "Yes, I know of the fishtailed warrioress. I will seek what I can, Sage Onmai."

Smiling at the playful name coined for her pupil, she releases the young one. "Well then, be off. Remember, keep your head up, for you never know where trouble is lurking."

CHAPTER TWO

2

C lashing weapons and screams of mercy ring through the field as dirt and ash fill the sky and lungs of fighters trying to stay alive. Warriors fight through the weariness caused by the beating sun.

Stepping over bodies of fallen enemies and comrades, fighters push on. The air is salty with the stench of blood, and the ashes of burning cinders coat their tongues with each battle cry. Warriors breathe the acrid fragrance of smoke and carcasses, reminding them of their proximity to death.

Among those fighting for life is a warrior that towers over the slain. His broad shoulders heave up and down as he tries to force more air into his lungs. His gaze shifts from his front to his side, assessing the approaching enemies.

This warrior is Eli. Roaring, he takes his blade and slashes through a charging fighter. Blood flies, splattering across his face, but his opponent does not fall. Placing his hand against the bloody wound, Eli prepares to shoot a blast of air from his fingers. Letting out another battle cry, he releases a deadly windstorm that cuts through his enemy.

Mind and body dizzy with exhaustion, Eli watches his opponent's body fly across the battlefield and drop onto the muddy earth.

"Well done, my love, but watch your back," calls Talia, approaching her husband. Her fishtail braid flies as she launches her spear, stopping Eli's would-be attacker from charging his rear.

"My heart," he responds, reaching for her. Talia firmly places her hands on his chest.

"I do not want the blood of another on my lips," she muses. Talia removes her fingers from him and places them on her lips, then tenderly on his.

For a moment, the crash of bodies and the sulfuric scent of battle mean nothing to the two lovers. Their exhaustion wanes, fueled by the touch of each other.

"Are you hurt?" he asks, pushing her braid from her shoulder and exposing a fleshy gash on her bronze skin.

"No more hurt than you and nothing that requires urgency," breaking his gaze, Talia scans the battlefield. "We are pushing them back."

"Yes, but they still do not retreat."

"Small victories, my love," she says.

Before Eli can respond, the pounding of rushing feet and the glint of raised blades draws Talia's attention. Her rage is as ferocious as her passion as she steps beyond Eli. Talia pulls the water vapors from the air, trapping the two approaching warriors in a water bubble. The mercilessness of her gaze is the last image they see, as she keeps them immersed in her attack. Their knees buckle and their bodies grow still, as Talia drowns them on dry land.

Eli returns to her side and places a hand around her waist, steadying her weary body.

Closing her eyes, Talia breathes slowly, then pulls away. "Eli, I am fine. I'm more exhausted than I accounted for. We must use our elemental attacks sparingly if we are to survive this battle."

Looking around, he says, "We must either cut down every fighter or find their leader. If we are to end this."

"Good luck securing him. The scouts have had no success."

"I say we find him and bring the fight to him."

Talia's gaze turns cold. "Eli, be wise. Kral has never lost a battle."

"I am being wise. Talia, we can not keep up this fight forever. We need to end this."

"What do you suggest, husband? Shall we desert the battlefield and set off on an unsanctioned mission?"

"My heart, you have the best ideas," Eli replies, shifting his gaze behind her to quick movement at her rear; his breath quickens. Rushing forward, he drives his blade through the ambushing warrior's chest. Growling, he shoves the lifeless body from his weapon.

Breathing heavily, he returns his attention to Talia. His gaze brightens, seeing her unharmed.

"Watch *your* back," he muses.

Talia punches his shoulder.

"Ow," Eli rubs his arm, but does not let his proposal slip from their conversation. "Talia, the price of freedom depends on what we are willing to pay. I have no interest in paying for it with our lives or the lives of our children. Tell me, what is the cost of our people's freedom?"

Talia looks from Eli to the battlefield, allowing his words to chip at her apprehension.

"Eli, we are supposed to follow orders."

"Our orders are to win the battle, my heart."

The cries of exhaustion and death fill their silence. Ox Nation pushes closer to the village where their children lay their heads. Zodian fighters rush to push Kral's forces from the front lines.

Seeing her children so close to danger, she rids herself of any remaining doubt, "Fine. But if we are to embark on this task, we will need someone skilled in tracking."

"Sumarra?" he groans.

She smirks, "Her scouting skills make up for her nosy nature. If we can convince her, we may have a chance."

"Where is she?"

"They are keeping the scouts near the campgrounds. If she is not hunting Kral, she will be there."

"Go," he instructs. "I will do my best to clear a path. The Ox Nation is coating the rear battlegrounds. If we get separated, meet me past those trees."

Talia nods, and their mission starts with Eli stepping forward, cutting down anyone who would dare block their path.

Chapter Three

3

Past the sea of fighters crashing closer to the village gates are sets of tents. Talia steps into a scouting tent that is mostly bare, save for a few resting warriors. The scent of lemon balm permeates the air, signaling the need to quell anxious warriors to rest. Talia hears the resounding sounds of war cries, footsteps from the tents where sleeping warriors lie. As she looks over at the resting scouts, she listens for the sound of Eli not far behind. Her instincts as his lover and war partner urge her to fight at his side, but she wrestles against her nature, knowing she must seek Sumarra.

Talia moves about in war-torn clothing. She does not look out of place from the scouts clothed in their own bloody garments. Recon has not gone without bloodshed and loss; she gathers from the piles of bloody clothes and empty cots.

They have combined two tents to make one large section of sleeping quarters. Talia pulls back the green flap, entering the second tent. When she steps through, she releases a sigh. In the back is a single person. A small woman, who almost blends into the muted green of the tent with her dark clothing and deep brown skin.

"Sumarra," she whispers.

Sumarra turns and faces the fishtailed warrioress. She waves Talia over, and she crouches beside the cot. When Talia is at Sumarra's side, the wear of battle becomes more evident. Dirt and ash cover Sumarra's face. She carefully applies a creamy paste to her foot. Gingerly, she works the remedy over her sore soles, and her petite frame relaxes in relief.

"Comfrey?" Talia asks, pointing to the purple specs of flower.

Sumarra offers a fatigued smile as she rubs her reddened and calloused foot, "Yes. But don't tell anyone. I've been making a small batch of comfrey ointment when I find the flowers. These scouting trips keep getting longer, and my feet ache. How am I to find a lover like yours with poor feet?"

"If you find one like mine, it won't be your feet that keep him satisfied."

They chuckle softly, careful not to draw attention to themselves as someone walks in and lies on an empty cot. The person turns their back to the two women. Sumarra and Talia wait for the person to settle. They hear the soft wheeze of snoring moments later.

Talia moves to the cot, sitting beside Sumarra, and lowers her voice. "I am not here for your fresh banter. I have a request."

"What is it?" Sumarra whispers back.

"It is a fool's errand."

"I told you I am listening."

"It could be treasonous."

"Talia," Sumarra's voice raises, and the person's snoring stops. The two women huddle closer. When the person snores louder, Talia continues.

"Eli has a plan about how we can support the troops. He thinks we should search for the Ox Nation's leader, Kral. It is a fool's errand and a disobedient act. But something in that man is urging him to try."

"And you need me because I'm a tracker."

Talia nods. She accesses Sumarra, watching as she considers her words. The two women turn toward the sound of shouting outside the tent. It is a mixture of pleading and screeching that has become as common as the sounds of morning songbirds.

The sound edges closer, and their faces twist into pained grimaces.

"Those are the only sounds we hear upon our return. If it's not from our fellow warrior with half-burned limbs, it's from scouts injured from an ambush. This has to stop."

Talia listens to the quiver in her fellow warrioress' voice and knows it is not from fear, but sorrow.

"The front lines are closer to you now than to our quarters."

Sumarra nods, "Talia, I know the sounds of battle; you know I do. But I am tired of hearing the groans of my loved ones. Angered when I am filled with thoughts of what Kral's forces will do to those back in the village."

Talia grips Sumarra's hand. She squeezes her cold, wet fingertips. They listen to more sounds of pain and shudder as the voices abruptly go silent.

Sumarra turns to look at the sleeping person on the cot behind them. Shaking her head, she says, "There is no herb, nor ale that can make me sleep through those sounds."

Talia turns, watching as the body rises and falls. She marvels at how she has slept through this battle when Sumarra draws her attention.

"Eli, you said he needs help. I will do it. Whatever it is."

Filled with conflicting joy and pain, Talia looks deeper into her eyes, "We could be punished."

"We could be praised," she responds.

Talia hangs her head and shakes it, "I am surrounded by fools."

"You are surrounded by those needing an end to this tireless war. If Eli has a plan, I will gladly follow."

"Well then, let's be off."

They rise, ready to tiptoe from the tent, when Sumarra halts, "Talia, let me gather supplies. I've seen the terrain and think we need some items."

Talia's jaw tightens, "We should move swiftly."

"I won't be long. Promise."

They hear shuffling from the first tent as more people enter. Generals bark orders, and scouts rise from their cots. Fearful Sumarra will be called, she nods, "Fine, but be quick."

Sumarra smiles, and Talia instructs her on a meeting point.

"Let us pray to the ancestors that all will go well," Talia whispers.

"Un bebe de fae," Sumarra replies in their native tongue.

Talia grips the cloth of the tent. Before exiting through the flap, she whispers back, "Yes. The stars bless babes and fools. But let us hope we are the babes in this situation."

CHAPTER FOUR

4

Crickets sing, and fireflies signal night as Eli and Talia await Sumarra. Moss clings to trees, dampening the air as looming clouds signal rain. Talia rests her back against the rough tree trunk. The choppy bark presses into tender wounds along her back. Deeper she presses into the sturdy trunk; the piney scent lulls the tension of battle away from her body. Her eyes drift shut, but Eli's heavy footfalls distract her from sleep. Glancing his way, she observes his steps, creating a path that mimics the crease between his brows.

"She will be here, Eli. Be still."

"We could miss our chance if we wait."

"We do not know what we are doing, so we may miss our chance either way," says Talia.

Hearing the grogginess in her words, Eli turns to her. Talia's eyes lightly flutter shut and open. Smiling, he directs his movements to join her.

Birds perch in the trees, rustling the branches, as if war is not raging nearby. Their calming chirps create a normalcy that the two lovers have almost forgotten. When the wind blows, it causes Talia's braid to graze the back of Eli's hand.

Warmed by the unexpected touch of her hair, he reaches for it. Running his hand through the end of her braid, his fingers wrap around the tuft of her soft hair. As his fingers stroke, he feels the roughness of matted streaks of blood locked in between her strands.

Drawn by his hand, Talia turns to his touch.

"What do you think our children are doing?" she whispers.

A smile tugs at the corner of his lips at the mention of their young ones, "I am sure Alora is keeping the rest of the crew in check."

Talia groans, "I pray the four of them are not tearing the encampment apart."

"Let us hope we find out soon."

A branch snaps and birds flutter in the distance.

Eli and Talia shift from being loving parents to protectors, ready to fight. The rustling of the brush increases in speed, and their bodies fill with urgency. Standing side-by-side, they ready themselves for battle, tensing their fingers around their weapons in preparation. As the clearing grows wider, they relax their stance, though their irritation remains.

"Sumarra," Talia growls.

"Why is she not alone?" Eli grumbles.

"You said you were grabbing supplies, not people," Talia snaps.

"What's a mission without a few companions?" calls Veya, following Sumarra. Corrine, behind the two, stands taller and broader.

"If you all wish to stand a chance, you will need a warrior with my strength," says Corrine.

Corrine flexes the muscles of her broad shoulders.

"Careful, Corrine, we don't want Eli getting jealous," Veya teases.

Her comment stirs laughter from Corrine and Sumarra, while Eli folds his arms.

Their laughter is loud, but not louder than the war drums beating faster and louder in the distance. It is the roaring call for more troops. It is the sound that makes their lighthearted banter seem juvenile, stirring Talia to anger.

"This is no game. If we fail, a lashing or worse lies on the other side of this," Talia pauses, allowing her words to resonate. "If this is your choice, be sure."

Sumarra, Corrine, and Veya stand shoulder to shoulder, unwavering from her words.

Sumarra, the smallest in stature, has a mighty determination in her eyes. Veya, the most youthful of her peers, stands ready for warfare. Corrine, who has the size and strength of the greatest of warriors, does not falter at Talia's warning.

"I think I speak for all of us when I say we are tired of losing to these troops. This is our homeland. We are ready to bring the fight to Kral," says Corrine as Sumarra and Veya nod in agreement.

Talia pinches the bridge of her nose as she looks at the three women.

"We are all fools," whispers Talia.

"Not fools, my heart, but warriors determined to save our homeland."

Talia narrows her eyes, a chilling expression that does not steal Eli's vigor.

Turning to him, she encourages him to continue, "Well, this is your fool's mission. Shall we begin?"

Eli squares his shoulders, "Let's begin."

CHAPTER FIVE

5

Taking the lead in the strategy, Eli asks, "What has everyone heard so far? We can use what we know to direct our path."

"I heard we lost another scout unit a day ago near the Canary Mountains," says Veya.

"Yes, but when they sent us to investigate this morning, we came up empty," says Sumarra.

Talia responds, "Today, many of his warriors had damp clothing and smelled of cinnamon."

Corrine steps forward, "There are many Camphor Trees, which smell of cinnamon, near the Golden River. It rained in that region last night."

"Good," Eli begins. "If we believe, Kral directs his troops from his last meeting place. Is there a pattern with his previous locations?"

"This might help!" exclaims Veya, holding up a folded piece of paper. "I borrowed a map from the general's tent."

"Veya!" they shout.

"I'll bring it back."

She opens the paper, holding each end with her hands. The map is of Zodia and spans Veya's entire body. While not as petite as Sumarra, she is almost too short to hold open the map.

"The generals have marked where scouts have died. We will call those Kral sightings. What are these markings?" Talia asks.

Eli, Corrine, and Sumarra look closer. "Blockades. I was on the scouting team that encountered a block here," Sumarra points to a region on the map. "The blocks are everything from fallen trees to shifts in the land."

"Why use energy doing that?" Talia asks.

"Because they are moving here. Just beyond the Elders' Villa. We think we are pushing them back, but we are moving away from the Elders. If they attack from behind, we will be too far to get back before they overtake the village," says Eli.

"We will be too far and too tired," corrects Talia. "The battle has gone on too long. We have to assume Kral has enough warriors with him to overtake our village."

"A village with no warriors in it, except for the sentries guarding the Elders. If we can get to Kral and his troops, the five of us may overtake them," says Veya, peering over the map.

"If we make Kral our target, it could work. We must make sure we secure him," Corrine says.

"Should we focus our attention behind the village?" asks Sumarra.

"We can not be sure," advises Corrine. "The scouts have all died before intel has reached us. No one can confirm he is in those locations. They could be factions of his troop or his correct position."

"What have we to lose? This is all we have right now," Eli presses. "If we can narrow a likely location, we can have Sumarra use her abilities to search the earth in that region."

Veya closes the map and joins the huddle of the four, searching for answers.

"The scouts have tried searching the earth's energy; it did not work. We think his elemental fighters are manipulating the energies somehow." Responds Sumarra.

"Maybe that's the key," all eyes shift to Eli.

"What?" Talia pushes.

"Sumarra, search the earth for disturbances. That might help us pin down a location."

"There are disturbances everywhere. This war hurts the Earth, and it cries out in pain. It hurts for us to search its energies for answers, and it takes too much of our strength. Why do you think we have been searching less frequently?" Sumarra shudders at the request.

"I know," Eli pleads. "We need you, an earth elemental, to connect with the flow of the land. We are looking for energy that feels different. That feels manipulated by some other force."

Veya places a hand on Sumarra, "Draw from me to help balance the drain."

Looking into the agonizing faces of the others, Sumarra agrees.

Bending to the earth, her hands reach into the soil. Squeezing her eyes shut, she winces against the pain.

"The Earth is in such torment," she quivers. "I want to pull away. I have to separate myself from its energies."

Veya's fingers grasp her shoulder, "I'm right here. I'll be the tether drawing you back if you go too deep."

Sumarra nods, seeping her presence deeper into the earth's roots until she feels the area around the village.

"I feel the buzz of our people in the village. I'm trying to push past, but something is blocking me."

Eli, Talia, Corrine, and Veya look at each other.

"It could be Kral," breathes Talia.

Eli leans down, "Sumarra, what about the animals, trees, the earth? If they are making a blockade, they will have shifted one of those."

Sumarra says nothing but nods. Sweat forms around the nape of her neck, causing her coils to curl. Just as she moves to pull away, a flicker of energy catches her attention, drawing her to the very thing she has been seeking. It is a rushing sensation of the mountain stream and the shriek of fallen trees.

"There!" she shouts. "Where is the map?"

Sumarra stands, then stumbles to the ground. Veya supports her while Corrine opens the map. Sumarra steadies herself. Pointing to the map, she exclaims. "Here. I think this is where he and his troops are located. I could feel the earth shifting and trees calling out for their brethren."

"Kral is most likely there," Corrine says.

"Agreed. That vantage point has the best tactical advantage in over-taking the city while we are far from intervening. Sumarra, do you have the strength to move?" Talia asks.

"No. I don't think I would be much help."

"I will stay with her for a bit. Then we will update the generals. We will be with you within the hour if they have not locked us away for our disobedience," Veya says.

Eli, Talia, and Corrine do not falter at the thought of punishment as adrenaline buzzes through their body. As if stirred by their energies, the wind whips quicker, causing the trees to dance and hum.

Looking from Corrine to Talia, adjusting their weapons, Eli asks, "Shall we?"

Talia unsheathes her blade, and Corrine adjusts her quiver.

"Alright then. I will portal us to the area above where Sumarra showed us. We will come down and ambush their forces."

Nodding, Talia and Corrine prepare themselves.

Eli draws the energies from the air. As he pulls from nature, sparks flicker, and the wind snaps like the crack of a whip. The particles fuse, casting a white light over them. Sending a waft of cool air over the warriors, it opens. On the other side, sunlight filters through the dense thicket of trees and mountainous forest, revealing an undisturbed terrain untouched by war.

"Good luck," calls Veya over the windy sound of the portal.

Pushing past the beating wind, the warriors step through to face the unknown, leaving Sumarra and Veya watching as the portal phases away.

Sumarra and Veya remain grasping each other as the dust settles.

"They'll be okay, won't they?" Veya asks, clinging to her friend.

"For all of our sakes, let us hope the three of them will be enough."

CHAPTER SIX

6

S tepping through the portal they enter a land untouched by war and carnage. The scent of lavender coats the air, and flowers do not have the stain of bloodshed. Branches are free of ash and soot, and the air is not heavy with the metallic tang of blood, yet the three warriors can still detect the sour scent in their nostrils and on their tongues. War is on the other side of the village, but not far from them as they step forward.

As the light from the portal dissipates, Eli, Corrine, and Talia allow their eyes to adjust to the dimming light of late afternoon.

Corrine steps in front of the others. Turning her head, she listens to the bareness of the forest, "Are you sure Kral and his forces are nearby? The land is too quiet."

Eli does not waiver under the weight of her scowl.

"Let us travel further down. Corrine, are you able to sense anything in the land?" he asks.

"I am a fire warrior, Eli. I would be better tasked at setting this place ablaze."

Straining to look beyond the trees, Eli gestures forward, "We should move. Soon we will lose light."

Corrine and Eli step forward. When he does not hear the third pair of footfalls, he turns to Talia.

Corrine and Eli slow their movements and observe Talia. Her eyes are closed, and she seems as peaceful as if she is sleeping. The only sign of her awakened state is the twitching of her fingers.

"I can not search the earth for Kral's movements. But if we can find water, I can search the current for disturbances," Talia informs them.

The broadness of Corrine's shoulders drops, and Eli smirks sweetly.

"You never cease to amaze me, dear one."

Talia opens her eyes, "I hear the bubble of a brook. I need to get closer, and I can use its flow to take stock of what is happening in its path."

Fueled with eagerness, they make their way deeper into the forest until the sound of the rushing stream is as loud as the birds overhead. The crisp clear waters rush between rocks in its path.

Talia reaches into the stream. Shivering against the rush of coolness, she braces herself as she glides her hand deeper into the stream.

"What do you feel?" Corrine asks, unable to hide her anticipation.

Talia allows her senses to push past the cold until she fuses with the current. The coolness becomes a part of her being as she sinks deeper into the stream's energy. She flows through the forest with the rush of the current until she experiences a disturbance.

"They are there," her eyes dart to Eli and Corrine. "You were right, my love. Kral and his men are down the stream. Possibly preparing to rest for the night. I can feel their vibrations and movements as they take from the brook."

Talia removes her fingers from the water and rubs them together to warm them. Eli wraps his hands around hers, sharing his warmth.

Turning to the two lovers, Corrine lightly taps the handle of her dagger that is tucked in her belt, "We should wait for the generals to send sentries our way before we proceed."

"Corrine, we cannot be sure they will send anyone. The battle has stretched the front lines thin. And any deviation from their current position can signal we are on to Kral's strategy," says Talia.

"It's up to us," Eli begins. "We will have one shot at this. Our plan remains the same. Sneak up, grab Kral, and portal to the Elders. It will allow them to negotiate an end to this war."

"I believe, like Eli, that this is our only hope of ending this," Talia says.

Eli and Talia rest their eyes on Corrine.

Holding their gaze until she declares, "Onni Boa May Lei."

Lifting their head in honored agreement, Talia repeats the spoken words of their native tongue. "Onni Boa May Lei. May the ancestors welcome our spirits."

"But let us hope we don't meet tonight," calls Eli, breaking from Talia's fingers and toward the looming battle.

CHAPTER SEVEN

7

Breaking from spoken words, they communicate and signal their direction using hand movements. The encampment is still out of sight, and the sun has already sunk below the horizon, making it hard to make out any shapes. Slowing down their pace, they allow their other senses to take over and guide them forward.

Knowing Kral's forces will outnumber them, Eli signals for them to widen their distance, allowing them to sneak in at different points. A strategy, he prays, will increase their likelihood of catching Kral if they capture one or more of them.

Closing into their target, they hear the rumble of hushed voices. The camp comes into focus for Corrine first, who signals that there are ten warriors in the camp. Talia and Eli wait for her to signal that she has seen their target, but she motions back. Kral is not in sight.

Talia crouches lower as she moves closer to the tents. The sun has set, but the full cover of night is not yet upon them. She moves, hiding in the shadows as she disappears out of sight.

Eli, who is furthest from the camp, watches as Talia slips into a tent. He shifts his attention to Corrine, who moves like a panther stalking its prey in the night. Preparing to enter from his side of the camp, he halts his movements. A voice approaches. Shifting away from the voice, he shields himself with the tree trunk.

The voice grows louder; then, a body comes into focus. The voice towers over Eli. Scanning the man, he glimpses a knife hanging from his waist. It swings, thudding against the man's thigh. The sheath is as wide as Eli's hand and long enough to pierce his heart if his movement isn't quick.

Following the man, he stays within the cover of the trees. The man stops. Eli assesses the man as he relieves himself.

His instincts tell him to move swiftly as he draws the blade close to his chest. Offering a prayer he closes the distance. Darting from the tree, his blade presses against the man's throat. Eli's blade is sharp, and his movements are quick.

Deeply, he drags his blade against the man's flesh. The man recoils against Eli, but it is too late. Blood sprays from the fatal blow as the body drops to the ground. Eli steadies his focus and stills his shaking hands. Looking around, he ensures no one has heard the crash.

"Nine," he breathes, counting off the remaining warriors.

Pulling the lifeless body under the cover of fallen leaves and branches, Eli returns to the camp. His heart picks up pace with each stride, edging him around the makeshift camp. His vision narrows as his next target comes into view.

Taking cover behind a tent, he waits for the warrior to pass. Sneaking behind the warrior, a woman, he places his hand over her mouth. With his other hand, he grasps the top of her head. His opponent struggles, but only for a moment. Eli twists her head, snapping her neck.

He does not allow the body to fall, fearing it will alert the camp. He drags the woman, storing her out of sight. Before departing the tent, he glances at the body. The woman's build is like Talia's. Eli reminds himself that Talia is a formidable warrior and pushes away the throbbing sense of concern.

When he emerges from the tent, movement stirs him to draw his blade. Eli stills his hand as Talia comes into focus.

His heart skips frantically as he points to her blood-streaked shirt, but Talia shakes her head, signaling that it is not hers. He reaches for her hand and squeezes it tenderly. Breaking away, Talia signals she has killed three fighters. Eli signals he has cut down two. Leaving five plus Kral if Corrine has killed no one.

Talia signals to a tent that she has not yet scouted.

"What's the plan?" Talia signs.

"I will search out the tent. Seek Corrine and create a distraction on the other side of the camp," responds Eli.

Talia goes to move away from him when he grips her. The moment is fleeting, but for them, it feels like eternity. Talia places her forehead on Eli's, nudging him sweetly. He feels the dampness of her brow, soaked with blood and sweat. Eli inhales deeply, trying to detect her scent amidst the stench of death that envelops them. Finding it, he nudges her back, and Talia pulls away, disappearing once more.

Shifting away from passion and turning toward the adrenaline beating in his ears, Eli approaches the tent. His fingers tighten around the hilt of his blade. His hand grips the tent's flap when the sound of shouting and swords clashing draws his focus. He steps away to join the fight when he remembers his task.

"*Focus,*" he commands himself.

Moving to the tent, he thrusts the flap open, only to find it empty of his target.

CHAPTER EIGHT

8

Eli's eyes sweep across the empty tent, searching for the warlord, Kral, who is not in sight. Corrine and Talia's battle cries jolt him from his stupor. Racing toward the sound of combat, he assesses the scene.

Corrine creates a firewall, its blaze nips at the trees overhead. The massive wall creates a barrier between her and her opponent, allowing her to draw and release her bow. Cutting through the flames, her arrow pierces her enemy through his eye.

Before she can regain her breath, two more warriors are at her back.

Talia's cry draws Eli's attention to his left. Talia unleashes a barrage of attacks against one enemy, but it is the sight of her other opponent which makes his body grow cold. As Kral brings down his mighty blade, she nimbly escapes the swing of his attack.

Anger roars from Eli's lungs, shaking his body as he charges ahead. Before he can reach her, a chilling blast brings Eli to his knees. Grasping at his back, he cries out. A burning pain pulses through his back, churning bile in his stomach.

Being the wielder of such an agonizing blast, he rolls to the side when he hears the whipping sound of another incoming wind strike.

The blast etches closer, and he wraps himself in his own wind gust. The protective shield diverts the wind storm into a tent. A shiver runs through him as he watches the attack decimate the tent to shreds.

His sword is out of reach. Blown by the previous attack. He retrieves his dagger from the small of his back and regains his footing. Repositioning his weapon, he braces for his opponent's attack.

The attacker is an agile woman. Her movements are so swift they prevent him from taking the offense.

Talia wails.

Eli tries to face her, but his opponent's blade cuts through his side.

He growls, pressing his hand to his body.

His opponent snickers, "Best keep your eyes on me unless you wish to walk in the after realm."

Eli removes his blood-soaked hand from his side. He steps to launch an attack when his foe is on him once again. Her attacks are quicker and stronger than the last. Each swipe of her blade narrowly misses his vital organs. Fatigue causes his movements to slow, allowing her to land another attack.

Eli cries out in pain as his attacker gloats.

She draws back, ready to land her final blow.

Eli's world slows. The deafening sound of elemental warfare and the clash of metal rings in his ears. With each labored breath, his mind clouds, and instinct takes over.

He doesn't think, only reacts as the woman's blade stretches forth. Eli does not block her strike. His body braces for her attack.

Shifting away from his heart, he allows the blade to connect with his rib cage. Pacing his breath, he watches his wide-eyed opponent try to recoil away. Eli grips her wrist, preventing her from exiting him.

She tries to launch another attack, but his movements are fluid. In his free hand, Eli tightens the grip on his dagger. He plunges it into her heart and watches as life leaves her.

With his kill fresh at his feet, Eli pushes forward. Pain urges him to stop, but watching Talia's opponent wound her with another attack, edges him toward her.

Dragging forward, Eli cries out, drawing the attention of Talia's opponent. He locks eyes with Eli. The man wields a staff with feathers on one end and a blade on the other. The staffed warrior separates from Kral and Talia, pointing his weapon toward Eli.

Shifting to prepare for the attack, shooting pain reminds him of his injuries. He looks down at the blade still within him.

Bracing himself for the new wave of pain, Eli releases a guttural sound as the blade leaves his chest and thrusts the weapon at the man.

The warrior spins his staff until it is a blur, deflecting the blade. The blade ricochets from the staff and lands in the head of one of Corrine's opponents. Before Corrine's enemy drops to the ground, the man and his staff are upon Eli. Eli and his opponent enter a rhythm of swiping and dodging. Neither opponent loses ground to the other.

Eli's strength wanes. He lunges forward once, but his attacker evades and strikes twice. The second attack causes Eli to lose his footing. The man takes the feathered end of the weapon and drives it into his chest, forcing him to land hard on the ground.

The crash of the ground sends Eli into a daze. He tries to right himself, but the man is upon him. The staff comes quickly to his throat. Eli moves his hands promptly, creating a barrier between the weapon and his neck. However, the man uses his weight to press closer.

Straining to keep the man away, Eli feels the heat from his nostrils as the man inches closer. He tries to push, but his body is weak. The struggle causes his body to shake. The staff grazes his throat.

Eli prepares for the staff to crush him. His mind drifts to images of his children, held in his arms months ago. His memories fill with the sweetness of Talia's touch. As he readies himself for darkness, he hears the rumble of earth.

Shifting his eyes, he stares at the earth, shifting under Talia. Kral lifts his hand, displacing the deep roots of a tree. The movement brings Talia to the ground. Kral's blade glistens in the moonlight as he lifts it higher, ready to unleash his final strike.

"Talia!" Eli shouts.

Desperate for her, he uses his might to call upon the wind. Cultivating the powers of the air, Eli sends a powerful blast that connects with Kral. The attack sends him crashing into a tree.

Fueled by rage, Eli pushes back the man. He rolls on top of him, driving his blade deep into his chest. Dazed and delirious, Eli stumbles toward Talia.

"Talia, Talia!" Eli screams.

Wrapping her still body in his arms, his fingers cradle her head. He feels the warmth of her blood seeping from her skull. His chest burns, but then he hears the muffled groan trying to leave her lips.

"Talia," he breathes.

She tries to move her head, but he urges her to stop, "Don't move. Save your strength. I will get you to the healers."

Eli's mind cultivates the image of his desired destination; the healers within the Elders' Villa. Drawing her closer to his body, he vows to use his last drop of strength to get her to safety. His legs are shaky, but his determination is sound.

"Eli, no!" calls Corrine, still pushing back her opponent.

But her words mean nothing to him as he forces the portal wider.

Stepping through, Eli enters the healer's chambers, an area filled with the wounded. Healers run from one injured warrior to the next. Laying Talia on an empty bed, Eli cries out for help.

Talia's lips tremble.

"Shhh," Eli soothes, stroking her cheek.

"You're safe," he whispers as Talia's eyes flutter beyond him.

Turning to investigate the source of her fear, Eli finds Kral.

He reaches for his weapon but finds his sheath empty. His blade is on the other side of the portal.

Kral's blood-soaked blade cuts Eli across his chest. The strike brings Eli to the ground.

Blood soaks his shirt. His vision blurs as Kral's feet move past him. The pounding echo of feet fades as the pulsing of his heart fills his ears.

Screaming and pleading become fainter. The crash of glass feels as if it happens in slow motion. Eli tries to stir himself, but his body grows colder. The brightness of light grows dimmer. The pounding in his ears fades. Then the beating of his heart ceases.

CHAPTER NINE

9

His weightless body floats in a sea of darkness. Unable to orient himself, he clings to the sound of rustling fabric and the soft taps of feet. The gentle patter fills his ears, drawing him to his surroundings. Darkness fades, replaced by the horrific image of Kral and the glint of his bloody blade.

"Talia," Eli groans as a heaviness keeps him from rising.

He tries to shift, but pain and the unseen weight hold him down. His hands reach for his chest, trying to push away the source of the heaviness. His hands grip the figure, and a pleasant sigh leaves his lips. Resting his head on the pillow, his fingers lock around his youngest, Jane, resting on his chest.

He hears more shuffling. Straining to move, he tries to position himself to defend the resting little one, but he is too weak.

Eli grimaces and groans as his body protests his movements. Trying to rid himself of the dizziness, Eli rests his head on the pillow. A shadowy figure comes into view, and his finger tightens around his sleeping child.

"Rebellious one. Do any of you listen to me? I told you to stay off your father's chest," Talia scolds.

Eli's breath slows.

"Talia," he whispers, her name sweet on his lips.

She tries to move their child from him, but his fingers grip the little one. The weight is a pain he will take if it means he is alive and they all are safe.

"Kral," Eli's cracked lips croak.

"Shh," Talia soothes. "We can talk about all of that soon. But you are still weak, my love. Rest a little longer."

But rest, he can not. The footfalls beyond the door keep him from resting, and he has no desire to take his eyes off his love.

"This isn't the infirmary," he says.

"No, Eli, it's not. Rest. I will watch over you."

Eli's squirming rouses the little one, whose movements press deeper into his wound. He tries to stifle a groan, but he can not hide his discomfort from Talia.

"Enough. I will move Jane to your side. I don't need the others seeing her. They will only wish to climb onto you as well."

Eli, powerless to push back, submits as Talia rearranges their little one to his side. She strokes Jane's head, lulling her back into the dream world.

"Where?" Eli asks, more hoarsely than before.

Talia strokes the stubble on his face, then reaches toward a table that holds a glass and pitcher. She cradles his head before placing the glass on his lips.

The glass of cold water coats Eli's throat, forcing a cough from his lungs. Setting aside the glass, Talia responds to his question.

"You're in a secluded room in the Elders' Villa. I can only assume they are assessing your health while they decide whether to reprimand or commend you."

She pauses, offering him more to drink, when a figure stirs in the dark. Eli shifts his gaze, but Talia comforts him, settling his movements.

"It is only our other little ones; Alora, Tobias, and Ellie. They have been terrible without you."

A smile forms on Eli's lips, cracking them further.

Talia faces their children, revealing a patch of lost hair and a forming scab. His eyes widen, recalling the moments before the injury occurred. The memory causes a visceral reaction as he remembers the earth's vibration trying to swallow Talia.

"Your head," he calls, trying to reach for her. She grasps his hand, squeezing it tenderly.

"Looks worse than it is. The healers say your swiftness was my blessing. Your quick actions allowed the healers to ease the swelling before any damage occurred. I will be fine with rest, but with four under ten, I do not know how rest is possible."

"I am ten," groans a voice hidden under blankets. Eli beams, hearing the murmuring of his oldest.

Talia rolls her eyes, "You will be ten in a month, Alora. You are not ten yet. Return to sleep. It is too early to argue. Allow me another hour of peace before I must chase you demons around and nurse your father."

Alora giggles and settles deeper into the blanket.

"Sleep," she whispers into Eli's bright eyes, filled with love and passion.

"How long has it been?"

"Eight days," she responds.

He opens his mouth to speak, but the glimmer in her eyes silences his questions.

"I thought I lost you," she breathes, placing her hand on his chest.

They hold each other's gaze, willing their eyes to remain open, neither wanting to lose the other to darkness again.

The door creaks.

The sound pulls them from their embrace. When Talia sees the visitor, she stands.

"Greetings, Elder Onmai," Talia bows.

"How is our patient?" Onmai asks, pushing past the pleasantries.

"Dazed but awake," Talia settles beside Eli.

The children stir under the light filling the room.

"My apologies, dear ones. Did I disturb your rest?"

Before her children can get off a chiding remark, Talia responds, "No, Elder Onmai. They were just rousing."

Alora groans. Onmai chuckles.

"Well then, I have a treat," says Onmai.

Alora and her three siblings perk up and turn to the sage.

Onmai continues, "They have made me a mountain of food that I have not yet finished. Please help yourself with what I have left."

Talia cannot protest before the children have thrown off their blankets and appear at the door. Jane wiggles from her father's side and follows her siblings.

Onmai nods to the attendants, who take their places outside the door. Talia helps Eli to a sitting position as he tries to show reverence to the sage. She waves off his gesture and comes closer.

"Let me look at it," she says, pointing to his chest.

Moving, he shifts his robe open, revealing a wide slash that spans from his left shoulder to under his right rib cage. A deep purple bruise surrounds the salve that is applied.

"Well done. It looks like there is no infection. But you may have a scar that many will be in awe of for generations."

Grinning, he replies, "Thank you, Wise Sage. It will be a welcome reminder I am alive."

"You owe your life to Sage Onmai," Talia says.

Tilting his head, Eli shifts to view Onmai, who shrugs, "Your spirit was wandering between the lines of this world and the next. I only called you back, and you listened."

Eli tightens his grip around Talia, recalling the darkness, "I was dead. I died. The ancestors beckoned me to join them. It feels like a dream now. But I remember how close they were."

Eli's eyes dance frantically as he struggles to grasp what he thought was a dream.

Onmai rests a hand on his shoulder, calming him, "Rest your soul, Eli. You walked among the ancestors, but you do so no more. You owe me nothing. Your desire to live kept you tethered to this world. I only helped to direct you."

The memory of crashing glass and pleading causes his jaw to tighten, "Kral. What happened?"

Feeling Eli's body grow tenser, Talia shifts closer.

Onmai, whose face grows more solemn, speaks, "Your portal remained open, as I am sure you recall. Sadly, Corrine could not hold back Kral and his soldier with her injuries. They used the open portal to infiltrate our base. They killed many of those in our villa before being upon me."

"He reached you?" Eli questions, eyes wide with shame.

"Relax, Eli. I am still here with the living. But Elder Aster lost her life. The tales are true about Kral and his strength. He was formidable."

Eli shifts his eyes from the sage ruler.

"Eli," she calls. The sage's voice is tender and soothing to the pain filling his body, "You did a brave thing. While reckless, it might have been the only thing that saved my life."

His eyes shift back to the sage, waiting for her words to continue, "Veya and Sumarra's words did not go well when they spoke with the generals. When they mentioned the mission that was taking place, the generals brought their insubordination to my attention. To Kral's detriment, this meant our people were not as unprotected as he had hoped. Aster was the first to confront him and fell. But Kral didn't stand a chance against the generals when he encountered us."

"I wish I were on my feet to see Kral's head paraded through the troops," says Talia.

"No, Talia. We do not rejoice in death. There is already too much of that. We celebrate the end of an era of death," corrects Onmai.

"What of Corrine?" Eli asks as her words fill in his lost memories.

A smile returns to Onmai's face, "Kral's warrior injured her, but she is alive and will have the battle scars to prove her valiant efforts. When you were at Talia's side, she saw Kral rise. That is why she told you not to open the portal."

"I remember her calling out. So much is coming back to me. It's trying to fall in place, but it comes in flashes."

"Dear one, you should only focus on gratitude and rest. I did not stop by to fill you with worry, only to check on your progress. Rest. I will send for a healer to assess you." Onmai rubs her hand over Eli's face. He sinks into her strong touch. Onmai pats him tenderly before turning toward the door.

"Sage Onmai," Talia rises, halting the sage.

As if knowing the words about to be spoken, Onmai's tone turns sour, "Speak your mind, Talia."

"Since Eli is awake, will the remaining Elders wish to speak with him about punishment?"

Eli shifts, causing the bed to creak and his clothing to rustle. Onmai meets Talia's gaze, neither woman wavering.

Talia continues, "There are rumblings that there will be consequences for our unsanctioned actions. I would think those are only the words of those jealous of Eli's success. But I would like confirmation from you, Sage Onmai."

Talia bows deeply.

Onmai shifts, placing her hand on her hip, "You can save your performative respect, Talia. I have trained you long enough to know your ways."

Talia remains watchful as Onmai speaks, "We are a people that pride ourselves on order and discipline above all else. Eli and the lot of you disrupted order; therefore, you are open to discipline. I am sure you heard from Veya and Sumarra, who received their punishment. We have tasked them with cleaning the camps. But fret not. Eli has just opened his eye. I am sure I can stave off the remediation until he is on his feet."

Talia opens her mouth, but Eli's grip halts her.

Sighing, Onmai returns to a more agreeable countenance, "I think rest is in order for all of us. I will have my attendant return the children once they have eaten."

Talia offers her thanks, and the sage departs.

The door clicks, and the room becomes filled with the rushed patter of Talia's pacing.

"Sit beside me, my heart? You make me dizzy," Eli calls.

"I'm thinking."

"Talia."

"What?" Talia says in a tone that matches the intensity of her glare. Yet, her husband does not falter.

Eli extends his hand, easing her scowl.

"Must you be defiant?" he asks with a slyness on his lips.

Submitting to his pull, she steps toward him, "There was a time you told me you liked your women defiant."

He laughs, low and deep. The vibrations cause his chest to ache.

Talia is within his reach, and he wraps his arms around her waist. He closes his eyes and presses his face into her bronze stomach, breathing in the soft scent of lavender and shea. Drawing back, he welcomes the softness of her eyes and the gentle tracing of her fingers along his jaw.

"All will be well," he whispers.

Talia groans, "You always think so, but one day your luck will run its course."

Eli makes a tsk tsk tsk noise as he shakes his head, "Talia, as long as I have you by my side, I am the luckiest man alive."

She laughs devilishly, "If you weren't still wounded, I would illustrate all the ways that is true."

She kisses Eli longingly, and he sinks into the softness of her lips. He feels the warmth of her hands around him. Her touch and her presence warms him, but not in the way it had once before.

The thought is fleeting as the pounding of feet and banging on the door make him reach for the hilt of a weapon that no longer rests on his hip.

The door swings open, revealing the danger.

"Papa!" his oldest shouts.

"Move, Alora," Tobias scolds, elbowing his sister out of the way.

Talia steps away as each sibling takes a position on either side of their father.

Eli wraps his arms around his children, ignoring the soreness of his ribs so he can snuggle them close. Ellie returns, holding the hand of a young attendant, while Jane rests on the woman's hip.

"I hope they did not cause you much discomfort. They can be a handful," Talia jokes, taking the young toddler in her arms. Ellie removes her hand from the woman and wraps it around her mother's leg.

The attendant and Talia chat while Eli stares. He watches the gentleness of how she caresses the young one around her leg and cradles the youngest in her arms as if she did not wield a weapon with strength and ferocity with those same hands.

"Papa, are you ready to go home?" his son asks. Eli looks into Tobias' youthful eyes. Eyes unscared by images of battle.

"He will go nowhere until released by the healer," Talia instructs as the attendant leaves.

"What? I am as strong as an ox and ready to leave when I want," Eli says, flexing his muscles. His children gawk at his display.

"See, Mom, nothing can hurt Dad," Tobias responds, slapping his hand on his father's chest. Eli coughs and falters at the shooting pain radiating through him.

"Dummy! Why would you do that?" Alora scolds, swatting at her younger brother.

Tobias sheds his shame as he insults his sister and tries to avoid being hit.

"Enough, both of you!" Talia yells, trying to separate the two still clutched to Eli's side while her two youngest remain glued to her body. The arguing intensifies as blame shifts from sibling to sibling. The pain fades to a dull hum reminding Eli that he walks in the land of the living.

And for a moment, the proximity of battle and death is not at the forefront of Eli's heart and mind.

CHAPTER TEN

10

The welcoming creak of the floorboard and the nostalgic scent of soot and wood from the fireplace does little to ease the apprehension haunting Eli. Tobias and Alora charge past him, running to beloved hiding spots, yet the familiar patter of their feet and cascading pile of children's toys around the room do little to ease the desire to reach for his blade.

The floorboard creaks behind him, and Eli turns to the door where Talia watches him and the blade resting on his belt. She had inquired about the weapon before leaving the healers, but Eli insisted that its presence was necessary.

"Are you alright, my love?" she questions. "You seem lost."

His smile is reassuring as he kisses her gently, "I find myself looking for the smell of rotting flesh and metallic blood."

"Eli, this is not a battlefield. You will not find that here. Put that away. We are home now. Our days of battle are gone for now, even if it is, but for a moment," she says, reaching for the blade.

He twists his hip away from her reach, "The earth still burns with the cinders of war and the stench of decay. Such ideals as to relax are premature."

"Well, I will not wear it while I swaddle our young," she says, walking over to the couch where Ellie and Jane have settled.

Toy animals, play swords, and crumbled pillows fill the couch where the little ones nestle.

Their tiny eyes open and shut as they try to fight sleep. Wrapping Jane in her arms, Talia gestures for Eli to take Ellie. "Bring her to the bedroom. I do not wish to make two trips."

Eli wraps Ellie in his arms, drawing the little one close. Her weight is barely noticeable in his arms, unlike the broad sword he had wielded days prior. He follows Talia past the living space and into the back of the house, where the bedrooms and bathroom are tucked away.

Alora and Tobias' voices echo from a room down the hall. The thickness of the walls muffles the contents of their conversation but murmured threats of telling Mom and Dad ring loudly. Eli hears Talia groan, both of them wholly aware that one of the older siblings will ruin the nap in progress.

They enter the room filled with stuffed animals. The noonday sun casts rainbow rays through the window pane. Moving to the bed, Eli settles Ellie in her bed across from her little sister, Jane. The little one nestles close to her pillow, and Eli turns away from her.

"Where are you going?" Talia whispers.

"I am probably better served elsewhere."

Talia glares at him, "If you leave, she will demand my attention, and I will be stuck here for hours instead of minutes. Draw the curtain and sit."

Stifling a sigh, he closes the curtain and shuffles to Ellie's bedside. The little one snuggles close to the side of the bed, nudging her father. Eli feels the heat radiating from her body to his. He hears the hushed whispers and cooing of Jane fighting sleep that seeks to take her to the dream world. But Eli's attention is turned to the confines beyond the room. He strains to hear past the walls to what could be approaching. But he only hears the faintness of rustling trees dancing in the wind and song from birds flying in the sky.

"Papa?" Ellie calls, looking at her father. Eli brushes his hand over her face, trying to wash away the worry in her eyes.

Rather than being filled with the many memories of snuggling his little one close, his mind flutters to how easy it would be for an enemy to crush her soft skull.

The bed beside him creaks. Turning swiftly, he sees Talia stand. His mind had wandered so deep he forgot she was there. He feels the gentle pressure of Talia on his back, peering down at Ellie, who is now wrapped in dreams.

"Well done," she whispers in his ear. Tugging him to rise, Eli follows her to the hall.

The hallway is quiet of arguing and distractions.

"It seems Alora and Tobias have settled their squabble," Talia muses.

Eli stands close, but his mind is far from his wife's words. Wrapping her arms around Eli, she calls to him, "How are you, my love? You look worn."

Eli feels the way she gently avoids his scar, allowing enough distance between her and his chest. He wraps his arms tighter, drawing her to him, "I am well, but my strength is fading."

Talia kisses the fabric between his incision, "It has barely been more than a week since I almost lost you. I welcome the day it becomes a distant memory. A faded moment in time."

"As do I."

"Rest, Eli. I think that is what we all need after so long from home."

He fills his lungs with the comforting smells of home. It had been weeks since they breathed in the familiar scents of their own space. As the fight came nearer to the region of Zodia, the Elders ordered those in the outer areas of the town to seek refuge in the village center to prevent the forces from being spread too thinly. Talia and Eli are part of the Zodian army, and both had been called to the battalion area in the early days of battle, forcing the children to remain in the camps with the other young ones, with families on the front lines.

Neither Talia nor Eli could sneak away to be by their children's sides. Even with the youngest being only four, in the weeks that the battle was at the village gates, neither could leave the battle camps for fear they would be called for combat at any moment.

Now, in the confines and safety of home, Eli allows his touch to remain. Nuzzling the space between her neck and shoulder, he feels the beat of her pulse quicken. His hand travels lower, resting on her curves.

Talia tenderly whispers, "Rest, my love. There will be time for that later."

Leaving one last kiss on her neck, he leaves for their bedroom. As he opens the door, he is reminded of the nights filled with love and children hiding in their bed, sure that their mother and father would protect them from the monsters that lurked in the darkness. He scans the room with lotion and perfumes all in its place. The sheets are crisply tucked, and pillows fluffed, all evidence of his wife's diligence.

Removing his clothing, he lies in the comforts of their sheets, warmed by the sun streaming inside. From his vantage point, he can see the edge of the Crimson Sun. He watches as if it will move closer to the Rising Sun in moments. Fear grips him tightly.

He pushes his hands to his temples, trying to push away fear. "One battle at a time, Eli," he whispers.

Shutting his eyes, he tries to focus on the gentle creaks as Talia moves through the house, no doubt restoring it to pristine fashion. As sleep becomes heavier, fear leaves.

As sleep tries to take him, a sound jolts him awake. He focuses on trying to identify the nature of the disturbance, only to find that it is the sound of one of his children or Talia.

When Eli drifts off to sleep, his slumber leads him down a path of darkness and into a world of torment. His skin burns with fire and ice singed from a wind blast. Free from one attack, he faces another foe. Kral appears in the shadow of night, with his fingers burrowed into Talia's neck.

Ripping the sheets from his soaked body, Eli searches for a danger that only exists in his mind, yet he can not shake the vividness of battle, and the cries of pain that make his skin crawl.

With rest no longer an option, Eli heads to the single bathroom in a family of six. After multiple interruptions and pleas from children begging to use the bathroom, Eli emerges from a warm shower that leaves him feeling revived. When he exits, he finds Talia engaged in a history lesson with Ellie in the kitchen, while Jane plays on the couch with a doll.

Wedging his body in the door frame, he listens as Ellie recounts the story of the prophecy.

"The prophecy gets passed down from sage to sage through a dream. In the prophecy, the sage tells a story about a strong warrior from a faraway land. After years of using their prophecies and visions, the Elders have discovered the land where the Chosen One lives. Because of the visions of this world, the Elders can portal a Zodian hero to that world when the stars align."

Ellie pauses, waiting for her mother's approval. Talia nods, and she continues, "The prophecy is about a person who will be the strongest warrior. They will help us defeat the bad people that will appear when the Crimson Sun eclipses the Rising Sun. Mama, I don't remember the rest."

Talia strokes her head, "The Crimson Sun is our reminder that a battle is approaching. One more fierce than that of the Battle of the Ox. We search for this warrior that will defend us. While no one has found this person, hope remains. When the time is right, it will all come to pass. The prophecy says we will find the warrior in a place and time unlike any other."

Eli moves forward, filling his voice with bravado and using dramatic movements, "This fighter will wield power in a land without magic or abilities. It will happen in a time of great despair, when hope is only an ember. That is when one mighty traveler will see the strength of the Chosen One and be able to whisk them back to our world to aid us in the battle of all battles," he finishes theatrically, getting a rise of laughter from the little ones.

The laughter subsides when Ellie asks, "Mama, when will the Crimson Sun reach our sun?"

Eli and Talia look at each other, searching for a way to answer the unknown. Talia prepares to speak, but Alora talks, taking her place at the table, "No one knows when it will happen. But I hear it is moving faster than ever before. When we were at the camp, I heard the older kids say they think it will be upon us in a few years, so you better be ready to fight Ellie."

Ellie's eyes glisten, "Is it true, Mama?"

Ignoring her mother's scolding look, Alora continues, "You bet it's true. Look for yourself. It's closer now than it was a few days ago."

Ellie's lips tremble, "Is that true, Mama? Is it closer?"

A tear falls from her eyes.

"Alora," Talia growls, wrapping Ellie in her arms and stroking her head. Alora trades cockiness for fear when she notices her mother's face.

"I... uh...," Alora stammers.

Ellie whimpers and asks more questions about the pending battle. Questions that neither Talia nor Eli can answer.

"Ow," Alora groans, feeling the sting of a slap on the back of her head. She looks up to see her father glaring at her, sending an icy shiver down her spine.

"Not every thought should be spoken, Alora," he snarls.

Eli's voice rattles the walls and sends Jane sinking lower on the couch.

"Fear would do you some good, Alora. Do not speak callously of battle when you have yet to smell the stench of death or feel the blood hot on your face from your opponent. Perhaps when you have felt that, you will take heed of your words and not be so quick to scare your siblings."

"Eli," Talia warns, but her words do not reach him.

"Would you like to go to battle now, Alora? I am sure the maggots have yet to taste the flesh of those still on the battlefield. Perhaps we can even find the bodies left by those your mother and I have killed."

"Eli!" Talia shouts, tipping over the chair as she stands.

He snaps his head toward her, stopping as he sees her horrified expression. Turning to Alora, he sees her trembling hand. She slides it under the table when she sees his stare.

"I... I didn't mean. Alora, I am sorry. I don't know what happened."

The room grows still. Each child glances from their mother to their father. The bubbling pot breaks the tension. Talia picks the chair from the floor and tends to the meal.

The room defrosts from its frozen state, but Eli remains paralyzed. Talia orders the children to clean their hands, and they spark into action. Eli hears Talia's voice, but it is like he is underwater. Her words are too far to reach him. He feels her touch his wrist. He turns to her.

"Do you hear me?" the concern in her voice mirrors her gaze.

"What?"

"I said, let's not harp on what was. Just be more careful of your words," she repeats.

"Yes, I don't know what came over me."

"It's okay, my love. The battle is still with you. Give it another day or two, and you should be free. Now, come help me with these plates," she says, passing him tableware.

He falls into the routine of setting the table as the children argue about where to sit. The fighting ceases when Talia threatens no dessert. Eli joins in the conversation but feels disconnected from his body. It is like a scene on a stage. He catches an occasional glance from Talia, and he smiles back, trying to reassure her that all is well. He keeps repeating that he will be fine within a day or two.

But a lingering question throbs, dulling her words.

What if things only get worse?

CHAPTER ELEVEN

11

The house lies peacefully quiet as Talia stirs in the kitchen. The children rest soundly, lost in blissful slumber, but Eli stands guard at the bedroom window.

It's a moonless night, but the stars are plenty, casting an illuminating glow upon the treetops. Despite the stillness in the distance, Eli remains vigilant, scanning the shadows for any sign of movement. Time seems to blur as he keeps his eyes fixed on the window, never allowing his attention to waver.

"No sentries allowed in the bedroom," Talia calls from the door.

Eli glances at her, his eyes trailing up her legs to the towel clinging to her body. He smiles, but not in a way that reaches his eyes, before turning his attention back to the window.

He notices the weariness in his legs and the desire to lie on the bed, yet he needs to stand watch. To defend his family from lurking prey.

Talia shuffles closer and wraps her arms around his torso. Sighing, Eli relaxes into her.

"You will find nothing in those trees, my love. Kral is dead, and his warriors either killed or banished back to their land."

"How do you stop being on watch, Talia? You did so like removing a cloak."

She snickers as her kisses trail the hardness of his back, "I am a mother; our children won't allow me to remain on the battlefield."

His eyes remain fixed, searching for a danger that will never come. Talia moves to face him and takes Eli's face in her hands.

"It will get better," she promises.

The floor creaks under the weight of Eli's heavy foot as he wraps Talia in his embrace. They sink deeper into each other.

"You seem so far away," she whispers, feeling his warm kisses trail down her neck.

"I could never be far from you," his voice deep in her ear. She grinds her hips deeper into him. His desire grows with her touch.

"Talia," he breathes as he explores the depths of her curves.

"Eli," she moans as pleasure fills her.

The house's silence becomes filled with muffled moans and hushed whispers of lovers full of each other. Eli's hand moves over Talia's mouth, hiding her cries of passion. As their lovemaking progresses, Eli buries his mouth deeper into her body, hushing the moans escaping his lips.

When the night is late, and the lovers are satisfied, Eli holds Talia as she sleeps. Fearful that his dreams will rob him of his pleasure, he keeps sleep far from him. Pulling her closer, he feels the rise and fall of her breath. As his body mimics her movements, sleep becomes stronger. Sleep leaves and comes in flashes, as groans of a house at night rouse him. He stills his body with each sound.

His body sinks into sleep when there is another creak in the night. Eli listens as the sound creaks again.

In moments, he is on his feet. Drawing his blade, kept hidden under the pillow, he seeks the sound. Exiting the room where Talia lies, he moves without making a noise. His feet avoid the groaning floorboards as he moves toward the rustling. He stops. The intruder sounds again, this time revealing their location. They are in the kitchen.

Moving with purpose, he dashes around the corner to strike. With his blade raised high, he searches but finds no one. Heart pounding and ears ringing, he shifts to look around the room.

"Papa?" says a tiny voice.

Eli shifts his attention back to the kitchen, but turns his gaze to the floor. Ellie sits holding a cookie to her lips.

"Ellie?"

"Hi, Papa. Am I in trouble?"

Eli sighs. Resting his blade on the counter, he takes her into his arms. With his free hand, he takes a cookie from the glass covering that protects all of Talia's homemade sweets.

"No, little one. You are not in trouble."

"Then why did you look like you wanted to hurt me?"

He winces, wounded by her words.

"I heard a noise and thought everyone was in danger."

"Did you think I was a big monster?" she asks gleefully.

He chuckles, "The biggest."

She grins and growls.

Eli laughs and urges her to quiet herself, "We don't want to wake everyone."

Shoving the last bit of cookie in her mouth, she runs her fingers across her lips to seal them.

"Good, little one. Hurry to bed. Here, take my cookie."

Ellie's face brightens, and she squeezes Eli tight.

Leaping from his lap, she tip-toes toward her room when Eli calls to her.

"Ellie?"

She turns, nibbling on her treat.

"Let's have this be our little secret, okay?"

Finishing her cookie, she puts two thumbs up. Eli smiles, and she disappears behind her door. When she is out of view, his smile fades.

The house grows quiet, and he rises to retrieve his weapon. Taking it in his hand, he tightens his fingers around the hilt. With it in his grasp, his fear eases. While the shame of frightening his child does not dissipate, the blade is by his side as it should be.

Hallow and tired, he reminds himself of Talia's promise. Everything will get better. He just doesn't know when.

Chapter Twelve

12

The crowded market signals life is returning to normal following the war. Weeks have passed, and eager marketgoers haggle for the best prices as they try to refill their cupboards.

The village center is bustling with merchants on both sides of the narrow pathways. The aroma of rich spices and flavors causes mouths to salivate. People shout and push, trying to get what remains of the dwindling spices. Fresh vegetables are haggled for, like priceless gems, while those not brave enough to battle for these rare treats hide in the shadows, taking a reprieve from the beating sun.

The war burned many fields ready for harvest; hungry villagers are coveting what remains. Of those seeking to fill their pantries and bellies are Eli and his family. Talia is at the helm, pushing closer to vendors. As she steps forward, villagers rattling off numbers to get the best price push her further behind. As Talia attempts to get closer, Jane bobs up and down on her hip.

"Veyhere," Talia curses.

"Mom! That's a naughty curse word," Tobias snickers.

Talia glares at him, quieting the boy.

"This was not wise. The market is too busy. I can't get a word in. They will leave only the rotted and picked over when I reach the front."

"Dad is big and loud. He can do it," Alora says, pointing to Eli.

Eli stands in the rear with Ellie perched on his shoulders, trying not to push back as the crowd rubs against him. He woke up scowling, and his frown only deepened while being in the market filled with yelling and shoving.

Talia turns to him, assessing his glazed expression. Eli sees her concern as Talia tries to shuffle to another stall, "What do you need, my heart?"

"Nothing. Let's push on."

"Talia," he pleads.

Sighing, she turns to him.

"We need to get to the front so we can get anything at this point."

"Mama needs someone big, Papa," Ellie says, dancing on his shoulders. Eli bends for Ellie to take the bag of money from Talia.

"Alora, come. You have the basket. Stay close," he instructs.

"You got this, Dad!" Tobias chants as Eli steps forward. Alora follows close to his side.

Eli stumbles as someone tries to push him out of the way. He glares at the man, who scurries out of sight. Eli pushes forward, and Alora squeezes through the gaps. He gets a few shouts and stares that quickly disappear when they see his considerable presence.

Once close to the front, he shouts above the patrons, "Eh! You fill this basket, and you get what's in the bag. All of it."

The shopkeeper fixes his eyes on Eli. Whether Eli's offer or his demeanor, the man gestures for the basket. Alora shuffles forward, watching as the man fills it. She returns to Eli's side with the contents overflowing.

When Alora is back at his side, he says, "Good. Stay close and try not to lose anything in the shuffle."

"I can do that!" Alora shouts, ready to master her assignment.

Eli engages in pushing and scowling people from his path until they are back at Talia's side. Seeing the contents of the basket, Talia beams.

She assesses the items and nods, "I can do much with these. Well done."

"Do you need anything else?" Eli asks.

"No. We still have dried fish and meat at home. As for herbs, I can use some of the vegetation growing along the forest's edge. We can go home now."

"I would like that," Eli sighs.

They maneuver beyond the shops to exit the village with ease. Almost at the gates, they see Veya waving at them.

"Mama, it's the woman with painted skin," says Jane, pointing to Veya's white patches of flesh.

"That is Veya, and her skin is not painted. She has a loss of melanin on parts of her body."

Jane attempts to say the big word but fails. Tobias taunts his sister, and Talia glares at him to stop before the little one cries.

"Happy to see you two off the battlefield. Talia! Look at how big your little ones are. How old are they now?"

"Alora, my oldest, will be ten in a few weeks. Tobias is seven, Ellie is five, and Jane here is four."

Talia rubs her hand over Jane's braids, and the little one snuggles closer. Veya gushes.

"You and Eli make adorable children. Can we expect more?"

Eli groans, and Talia rolls her eyes.

"Hopefully not soon, but we should be going," Talia tries to push forward when Veya stops her.

"Hold on. Corrine and Sumarra aren't far, and we have news about your punishment."

Talia and Eli glance at each other. Ellie wiggles.

"Papa, are you in trouble?" Ellie asks as Veya clasps her hands over her mouth.

"How stupid of me. I didn't think."

"All is well. Alora, take your siblings to that bench by the fountain. You may play there, but do not roam from my sight. Do I make myself clear?"

"Yes, Mama," they all say, cowering under the power of their mother's voice. Eli kneels, and Ellie slides from his shoulders. The siblings follow Alora as she leads the way, carrying Jane on her hip.

"Where are Corrine and Sumarra? I want to know what you have heard?" Talia breathes. Her words are rushed, and her voice is raised. It is a tone Eli has heard on rare occasions when Talia is concerned.

"We are here. How's it?" responds Sumarra with Corrine at her side. Corrine wears a white paste on her neck, trailing down to her shirt.

"Corrine, how are you? We heard about your injuries," Talia says, embracing her fellow warrioress.

"Looks worse than it is. Kral's warrior got me in my neck. Besides the shooting pain, when I turn my head, I am fine."

Talia smiles. Eli remains quiet and assessing at her side.

"I was telling them we have news about their punishment," Veya says

Sumarra speaks, "Not news, but more rumor. When Veya and I were on tent cleaning duty, we overheard conversations. Many are upset about the loss of Elder Aster and think they should punish Eli for his disobedience."

"An act that saved all of us," Talia interrupts.

"Well, that is not how it is being described. There is talk of banishment. Elder Aster was beloved, and Eli... not so much," Veya says, looking from Eli to Talia.

Scowling, Talia replies, "Your feud with Gaia is no doubt the fuel for this. He would do anything to get back at you."

"That was ages ago, Talia," he responds.

"Apparently, not long enough," Talia says.

Corrine leans to Sumarra and asks, "What is the story between Elder Gaia and Eli?"

Sumarra whispers, "Well, when Gaia was seeking the Elder seat, he wanted Talia's hand in marriage. She was the best in our ranks, and you know how Gaia loves the best."

Corrine snorts, "Ida wanted Eli for the same reasons. That's why Talia can not stand her. She wanted to be with the best, but Eli was set to marry Talia."

"Do not speak of that witch in my presence," Talia growls, silencing their whispers.

"You will hear much more of her," begins Veya. "The Elders speak of giving her more authority for her work of magery during the battle. Ida's salve saved many warriors and helped to heal Corrine and even Eli," she says, pointing to the paste.

Talia turns her lip up in disgust, "Nothing good can come from her."

"They are calling her potions and abilities the best seen amongst our people in many ages," says Corrine.

Talia's jaw tightens, "They praise her while they punish us. Is following orders that important to our people?"

"As important as honoring the prophecy," says Sumarra. A heaviness falls on the five of them. Talia's gaze shifts to her children playing around the fountain.

"Do you know when we will hear about a decision?" Talia asks.

Sumarra speaks, "I have only heard whispers. But I feel it will be soon. I believe they wanted to assess the depths of Eli's actions and finish breaking down the war grounds before tackling a fresh problem."

Veya chimes in, "Sumarra and I will finish our duties in the coming days. Corrine has heard about her consequences."

Corrine speaks, "I am to handle the dirty work for the generals as they instruct the new trainees. I am sure the two of you will hear the outcome soon."

Talia shakes her head furiously, "They would be a fool to banish any of us. Especially Eli. I will not worry myself with rumors. Thank you for the information. We will be off and see what the coming days offer."

Talia and Eli say their goodbyes and make their way to gather the children.

"What do you think, Eli? You are awfully quiet."

"What is there to say? As you said, they are only rumors. Let's wait and see what becomes fact."

Talia grasps his hand, halting them in the village square, "Eli, you haven't been yourself for days. I don't want this to add to your worries. All will be well. I know it."

Eli smiles and kisses Talia softly on her forehead, "You always watch out for me. What could I ever worry about?"

He takes her hand gingerly.

She squeezes it, "My love."

"My heart," he calls as they close the distance between them and their children.

Eli watches as Talia tries to corral their little ones. He keeps a smile pasted on his face, reassuring his loved one all is well. But that is far from the truth. The big man stands watchful and empty.

Eli longs to tell Talia the truth. He is not worried. He has been void of emotion for days. The news shared by the others did little to shift that. It only serves as a reminder that danger lurks all around them.

CHAPTER THIRTEEN

13

Days turn into weeks, and the spirit of battle remains with Eli. The land of Zodia enters its dry season, which does little to quell the insatiable anger brewing within Eli.

As heat fills his days with anger, torment haunts his nights. His dreams are coated with danger, forcing him to toss and turn. His movements are so disruptive, Talia trades their bed for the lone sofa.

On this day, Eli has tried to stay away from his family to avoid a morning filled with outbursts. The couch, hard and filled with the scent of his beloved, is his resting place. Laying on the couch, Eli hopes the daylight will keep away the dreams of misery and allow him a brief rest.

The rise and fall of Eli's chest slows, causing sleep to become deeper. He feels the intense sensation of losing control, which stirs fear in his soul. The ongoing tug of rest and consciousness draws him to a place of dream and remembrance.

The dreams transport Eli back to the night of the attack. He feels the heat of the humid air filling his lungs. The wetness of perspiration down his back sends a shiver through his aching body. The world slows as he recounts the moments before his blade rests against his opponent's throat. His ears ring with the sound of metal on flesh, like the sound of wind whistling sharply past his ear.

Eli feels the air leaving the man's lifeless body.

A scream rings in the night. He stirs, turning toward her sounds of agony.

"Talia," he feels the tightness of his jaw as her name leaves his lips. Turning, he searches through the darkened forest, but can not find her.

"Talia!" Eli screams.

Crows scatter, leaving the tree tops and blocking the light. The darkness swallows him.

Turning again, he searches for the light, but he is face to face with a bloody Corrine.

Fear grips him. He tries to step back, but Corrine reaches a hand toward him.

"Save me, Eli," Corrine begs, blood spewing from her neck.

He backs away. His heart pounds like the roaring war drum, signaling danger is near.

He runs further and faster, stumbling in the dark until he stands faced with Kral.

It is not the man that sends the cold wave of fear through Eli, but who the man towers over.

The warlord hovers over Talia. Fear is present in her eyes as she looks at her helpless husband.

"Save me, Eli," she pleads.

Eli runs to her. He tries to reach Talia before it is too late. But as he is within arm's reach of her, Kral's blade enters her heart.

"No," Eli groans as the blood trickles from her lips. He races toward her, grasping her body before it hits the ground.

"Talia," he moans, stroking her body. His fingers tremble against her cold skin.

Kral's body cast a shadow over Talia's face, stirring a rage within a broken Eli. He looks up at the tyrant, ready to attack, only to be met with Kral's bloody blade between his eyes.

"No!" Eli shouts to the empty room. He searches for danger but finds none. The pulsing heart beating in his throat forces him from the couch. Seeking Talia, he calls her, "Talia. Talia."

He rounds the corner and finds her rushing from their room.

"Eli, what is wrong? Why are you screaming?"

"Talia," he groans, wrapping her in his arms. He squeezes her tighter, feeling her warmth. Burrowing his face deeper, he wills her scent to become a part of him, to be the only thing that stains his memory.

"Eli, you are scaring me," she says, trying to pull from him.

He loosens his grip, "I just needed to know you were okay. I thought I had lost you."

Her face does not share his same concern. She draws away, "Eli, I am fine. We are all fine. You are driving yourself mad?"

He recoils at her anger, "Talia, I don't know. I keep feeling like something is going to happen. Something out of my control. My only desire is for you and our children to be safe."

"Eli, the battle is over. We won the war. You will drive yourself mad if you do not rid yourself of these feelings."

Eli's heart races faster. Her lack of concern fuels his anger, "You scold me for wanting to keep you and our children safe. Talia, you are a devout preacher, teaching our children of the Crimson Sun. You remind them of the prophecy and war, even when a battle is fresh on our heels. How dare you look down on me for my behavior when you have done far worse!"

Talia takes a step back, "Eli, you are not yourself. So I will ignore your words. But I caution you, back down before our children return to this house."

"And if I don't?" Eli growls.

Talia draws away, her body tensing in response to Eli's words. As his gaze hardens, her body shifts, preparing for battle. Both assess each other like warriors on the battlefield, not lovers quarreling. Talia fades from his vision as his body is transported to the battlegrounds. His fingers twitch, yearning for the blade in his back pocket. As the knob turns, and the clatter of noisy children fills the room, Talia returns to focus. But she is a blur as she moves past him.

Welcoming the children back from an afternoon of playing and chores, she keeps her eyes on him. He watches, mystified by her tenderness, wiping dirt from their faces, as if they were not almost locked in battle. Eli tells himself she is not the enemy, "Home. Safe. Home." He repeats, trying to clear the haze. Glancing at Talia, he sees her warning eyes. Eli steps forward, and Talia creates a barrier between her and the children. He stops. She is not the enemy, his mind repeats, and he backs away. With his body shielded by the wall. He leans against it, urging the pounding in his head to stop. Braced against the wall, he uses its firmness to steady his shaking body.

"ROAR!" Tobias shouts.

The playful act sends a fresh wave of fear through Eli, who can not separate the youthfulness of his son from the battle cry of an impending attack. Tobias yelps, wide-eyed and trembling, as Eli pins the boy against the wall. The boy no longer looks into the eyes of his father, but into the scowling gaze of a menacing warrior.

Too scared to cry out to his father and alert him of the pain he causes, Tobias remains frozen as tears touch his father's arm. The moment feels like an eternity, but is over in seconds when Talia is upon

Eli. Her eyes are vicious and threatening, like a warrioress willing to destroy whatever is in her path. It is the look she had cast upon many of her enemies before they took their last breath. Her arm presses into Eli's chest, forcing him from their son. Tobias slides to the ground.

Fatigue and anger leave his body, slowing the spinning in Eli's head. His eyes shift to Tobias crying and cowering on the floor, then to Talia, who keeps her body pressed to his.

"Leave," she snarls, quiet and deadly.

Struggling to breathe, unable to say a word, he nods, signaling his approval.

Talia moves her arm, waiting to see if he offers resistance. Offering none, Talia moves further away, allowing him to retreat.

Keeping his head low and away from his whimpering child. Eli walks by, his heart sinking as he sees Ellie, Jane, and Alora quivering in the kitchen, their eyes are filled with horror from the terrifying sounds they heard in the hallway.

Looking away from their gaze, he keeps his sight on his destination; the door.

Leaving, Eli attempts to flee the sensation of loss and isolation, but his steps lead him closer to despair.

CHAPTER FOURTEEN

14

The pulsing rays of the Crimson Sun beat down on Eli as he allows his feet to wander. He throbs, both from the pain he has caused and from Talia pressing against his wound.

As he stands on the doorstep of the one they call witch and sorceress, he doesn't know why he is there. Perhaps to obtain more salve that has bonded him together or to seek if her potions are as magical as the whispers claim.

While he does not know why his feet have brought him to Ida, he does not turn away. His fingers linger on the door, clinging to salvation that may be on the other side.

"No," he breathes, knowing to trust her would be unwise. Turning to leave, he steps away, but images of his frightened children and Talia's wrath halt him.

Unwilling to return broken, he raps on the door.

"Come in," she calls from the other side.

He places his hand on the knob and feels his heart skip faster. Ignoring his instincts, he presses forward.

Inside, he sees Ida settled in her chair. The room is dark, except for half-burned candles that cast a luminescent glow on her pale skin. The smirk tugging at her lips makes Eli's stomach churn.

Her stare is intent, like that of a huntress stalking her prey.

She leans forward, her movements clattering the bangles on her wrist, "I wondered how long you would stand behind my door."

"Hello, Ida," he calls, guarded by the entrance.

"Do you intend to stand guard for all of eternity?" her smirk widens as she gestures to his position.

Leaving the door open, Eli steps forward. Ida gazes behind him. "Are you afraid you'll need a quick exit? I promise I don't bite, much," she grins, and he catches the gleam of her teeth.

Eli steps forward but keeps his distance. His eyes trail to the open books on the table. He sees images of herbs and words too hard to pronounce.

"I hear whispers that your spells are the best in the village. Is that true?"

Ida lifts herself from the chair, "It depends on what you seek."

"I am not here for riddles," he watches as her hands graze bottles filled with dried animal parts and dead herbs.

"And I am not here for lies. What is in your heart, Eli? Tell me, does the great Talia know you are on my doorstep looking for me to nurse your wounds?"

"This was a mistake," Eli growls.

Turning to leave, his steps are few before he feels her grip on his shoulder. Pivoting, Eli squeezes Ida's neck. She gasps as his fingers grip her soft flesh, choking the air from her lungs. Looking into her eyes, absent of fear, he steps away. Turning from her, his hands rub his face as he begs the noise inside his mind to silence. His eyes burn as he closes them tighter, slowing his racing heart. He listens to the clink of glass as she removes something from a shelf.

As she nears him, he listens to her skirt rustle. Her touch is cool upon his face as she guides him to her. Ida directs his gaze toward the bottle, "This will cure the battle pains that remain within you. But only one question remains. How badly do you desire to be free?"

His heart races at the chance of salvation. Looking deeply into the sorceress' eyes, he speaks his truth, "I would do anything to rid myself of this pain and anger."

Her lips raise into a sinister grin as she pops the cork. Placing the bottle to her lips, Ida empties the contents.

Baring his teeth, he growls, "Witch, what game do you play?"

"I play no games. I only complete the last step of the potion. A kiss seals this remedy."

"You think me a fool?"

"I think you want to be free. If the price is too high, you can leave."

Ida gestures to the open door, but Eli does not move. He has no desire to touch the lips of the sorceress, but the promise of wholeness is too sweet to leave. Eli turns his attention to Ida, whose grin widens. Pushing past the bile in his stomach, he leans closer. With closed eyes, he inches near her mouth when her finger halts his movements. "This only works if you do it passionately. So make it count," she whispers.

Eli swallows hard, and he focuses on his reason for being; Talia.

Looking beyond Ida and into the past, he recalls a memory of when he held Talia. To a time when they loved passionately. His arm reaches around Ida, and she sinks into him longingly. Eli parts his lips and hears the rush of Ida's breath leave her as they come closer. His lips are almost to hers when a voice fills the room.

"Eli!"

His body stiffens under Talia's commanding voice. Dropping his arms, he steps away and turns to his wife; he aches within his soul when he sees the hurt behind her anger.

Talia's eyes pierce through him to Ida. Fingers twitching into a fist, she speaks, "Witch, you cross a line when you try to have what is mine."

Ida snickers, "Are you mad I am the one he needs?"

Reaching for the dagger on her hip, she steps forward. Eli crosses between the women and draws Talia outside. Shutting the door behind him, he hears Ida's cackling laugh.

Talia pulls from his arms, striking Eli in the face. The force of her attack knocks Eli against the door.

"Eli, you are more than dead to me. You are a vapor that never existed."

Chapter Fifteen

15

Disregarding Eli's presence, Talia marches forward. She ignores the desire to drive her blade through him as he desperately chases her. His pleading and explanations mean nothing, as she refuses to acknowledge his being.

Her anger burns hotter than the afternoon heat. Her pain is greater than seeing Eli lie lifeless on the healer's table, yet she marches forward, promising she will not allow him to see her hurt. She vows never to be vulnerable enough to be shaken by his actions.

Talia was afraid when she first left their home, unable to find her husband. A fear that brought her to moments on the battlefield when Eli was far from her sight. She searched until someone said they saw the big man heading in Ida's direction.

She knew their words were not true, but she headed there with a desperate hope of finding her love. Only to have it shattered when she saw him in Ida's arms. She has one job as a wife and a mother; keep her family safe. A vow she honors with her life, so why does Eli seek the solace of another?

Eli comes into her view, and she walks faster. She can not see him, nor his pain, without seeing her enemy, Ida.

Has she failed so much that he would seek another?

Talia's thoughts cause her torment, but not as much as the image before her.

She stops.

"Talia," he breathes.

Catching up with her steps, he realizes it is not his words that have stopped her. Following her gaze, he sees their home and the person on their doorstep.

The house casts a shadow over the yard as the sun hovers behind the trees. The sound of their children fills the air as it does every afternoon. Everything is in its place except for Elder Onmai and her guards.

"I suppose we will learn of our punishment," she says, watching her children dance around the sage.

Eli reaches for Talia's hand, and she pulls away.

She uses the motion to push forward. With each measured step, she pushes past the fear looming in her chest. If she is to protect her family, she must square her shoulders and sharpen her mind, as any warrioress does as she prepares for what is to come.

"Mama!" Ellie shouts, wrapping her arms around her Mother. "We have a visitor."

"I can see. What a surprise, Wise Sage. Had I known you were coming, I would have prepared our home."

"This will not be long, and I needed some fresh air. Shall we go inside?" says Sage Onmai, gesturing toward the door.

"Alora, keep your siblings outside," Talia instructs.

Alora nods, watching the sentries take their post by the entrance.

Eli follows and catches Tobias examining him. When the young boy meets his father's eyes, he looks away.

Tobias kicks at the dirt, waiting for the click of the door. But he feels his father's hand rest gently on his shoulder. Tobias turns toward Eli, who kneels to meet his son's eyes.

Eli says, "Tobias, I should not have acted as I did. I am sorry for frightening you. Can you forgive me?"

With his eyes wide and glassy, Tobias hugs his father tightly, and Eli squeezes his son.

"Are you ready?" Talia calls, beckoning for him to join her and the sage.

He kisses his son atop his head, ruffling his curls.

"Dad!" Tobias groans, pulling away from his father.

He smiles, though it does not match the brightness of his son's eyes. Turning from his children, he disappears behind the door, bracing himself for what fate has in store.

Chapter Sixteen

16

Moving toys from the couch, Talia offers Onmai a seat. The sage sits unbothered by the reminders of little ones and youth. Eli takes his place in the door frame, watching as Onmai declines Talia's offer for tea.

"As promised, I will be quick," Onmai says.

Talia takes a seat opposite Onmai, where she glances at Eli. Both see the pain of what is coming before her words reveal the devastating blow.

"Eli, I am grateful you listened to your instincts and located Kral. But your actions were not without consequence. We lost many good men and women, including Elder Aster. As much as I would like you to escape punishment, it is not our custom to let disobedience go unchecked."

"But, Wise One—" Talia interrupts, but Onmai speaks.

"Don't, Talia. Like the others, I will not overlook you for your part in this. You, Talia, will be part of my personal guard. Do not think that is a luxury. I will task you with extra training, which will include obedience. All of which will steal time away from your home. As for you, Eli," Onmai stops, steadying the quiver in her tone.

Eli's gaze drifts to Talia. He can see her jaw tighten as she keeps her focus just beyond the sage.

"We assign you, Eli, an assignment both for your bravery and your defiance. The stars will soon align, signaling the time for a portal to open to the other world. Eli, we task you with securing the Chosen One."

"No!" Talia growls. "A death sentence would be more merciful. You would send him on a mission from which no one has ever returned?"

"Talia," Eli urges.

Onmai waves his concern away, "Allow her to speak her piece, for if you utter a word outside this room, I will have your tongue, Talia."

Talia glowers at the sage, "Half of our forces would be dead and buried if not for Eli's bravery, yet you want our family to continue to sacrifice. I will not allow this. I will not allow my family to be divided."

"You will," Onmai growls. Her voice is firm with the power of her authority. "You will, Talia, because I say you will. Because this is what the Elders require. Would you rather he be banished from our ranks?"

"How is this any different?" Talia says, keeping tears from her eyes. "How is his departure to this other world any different?"

"Because if we banish him, we will kill him upon his return. If Eli returns with the Chosen One, we will welcome him with open arms and warm hearts. Tell me, which would you prefer?"

"I would prefer you give him a mission from which someone has actually returned."

Eli lies in the doorframe, unmoved by his assignment, as he watches Talia and Onmai lock eyes with each other. Breaking her gaze, Onmai turns to him.

"Eli, you can refuse. I would advise against it, but if you do, I can try to search for another option. But be quick if you seek accommodation."

"Of course he does. Don't you, Eli?"

Eli can hear the rush in her breath and the fear in her eyes as Talia turns to him. He can see her pleading for her husband to fight.

But, for the first time since he lie awake in the Elders' Villa, the warrior inside him is at rest.

For weeks, he has felt like he drifts in the space between this world and the after realm. But this news, this mission, stirs a fire inside him.

Onmai rises, smoothening the wrinkles of her robe, "Think about it. If you choose to fight this, be quick. The stars will be in the position in ten days."

Talia scoffs, "So not only do you force us to decide, at haste, you would have him leave on Alora's tenth birthday?"

"I do not determine the stars, Talia. I only read them."

Onmai leaves without goodbyes or warm gestures. The only thing that remains after she is far from their doorstep is the pain and anger that Talia releases on Eli.

CHAPTER SEVENTEEN

17

Talia waves to her children before closing the shutters. The love for her babies is the only thing keeping her fingers from Eli's throat.

"You are a fool, Eli," she breathes, closing the distance between them.

"Can we speak on this later, my heart? My head pounds, and I need rest," he says, moving from the doorframe to the couch.

"Yes, my love," her tone sour, "we can speak of this another time. When you stand face to face with the portal, would that be a better time?"

"You are being emotional," he says, laying on the couch as if his wife is not at war with him.

"And you are being a fool. You have been one ever since our return home. You scold our son for his playfulness, nearly frighten Alora, then I catch you in the arms of that vile witch. And now, I see you entertaining, leaving us to hunt the Chosen One. A person no one has located. Was nearly losing us once not enough? Do you long for us to be apart, with such a desire, that you would embark on this impossible mission? Has our love grown that cold? Because Eli, if it has, I would rather you be alive and happy than alone and suffering. But perhaps love has made me the fool."

Standing before Eli, Talia bares her soul with open arms and a lovesick ache. Eli looks at the woman he has tied his soul to. A woman who has taken his breath with a mere glance. The woman who bore the impact of a battle injury with less agony than she does standing before him now. He watches as her body shakes with rage, and her eyes shine with tears. Yet, his heart has no affection for her.

Eli moves upright and looks into her eyes, "Talia, if our love were like water, I'd be drowning in it. You and our children are my everything. The desire to protect all of you burns in the crevices of my soul. But when I search for the warmth that our love once stirred, I can not find it. Talia, when I look at you, I only see your blood-soaked face and feel the coldness of death that was present on my lips."

Eli pauses, transported to when the staff lay on his throat.

"I don't know where the strength to move came from. All I know is I saw the ground almost swallow you whole, and that panic has not left me. That need to devour anything that would cause harm to you, or our family keeps me up at night. I feel that, but I can not feel the desire I once had when you lay next to me or whisper my name from your lips. I am sorry I disappoint you, but for the first time in many moons, I feel alive when thinking of a new mission."

Like a sail blown out to sea by the wind, Talia flutters to the ground, caught in the current of his words. Her compulsion to protect and defend her family is no match for the ghost of battle that still haunts her husband.

Eli rises. He walks, but not toward Talia as he once would have done. He passes her, heading for the door. When he reaches the knob, the faintness of her words stops him.

"So you will leave us?"

The wave of heat from the outside enters as Eli widens the door. Outside remains a peaceful contrast to the destruction that lies within the four walls.

Eli does not turn to her. He only confirms, "It's decided, but I think you and I knew that long ago."

CHAPTER EIGHTEEN

18

"Come on, Dad!" calls Tobias, running ahead in a game of chase.

"Quick, Alora. Go round and cut him off. He will not expect you at the stream."

With a wide smirk, she sets off in that direction.

Eli watches his children set off on two separate paths. Ever since Onmai's visit, his children have insisted on joining him on a training adventure. Today he obliges their request.

Tobias inches further away, and Eli sends an air current to slow his son. Tobias is prepared for his father's trick and uses the momentum of the elemental attack to fly high into the sky.

"Wee! I know your tricks, Dad," he shouts, landing on the ground.

His son smiles so that even Eli can feel the excitement buzzing within him. Eli calls Tobias, who dashes out of sight. Tobias dips through the trees and reaches the stream. Hiding behind a tree near the rushing water, he covers his mouth, shielding his snickering. He quiets himself and listens for his father's footfalls. The leaves shift, and branches snap as Eli approaches.

Absorbed by the sounds and sights in front of him, he fails to notice his sister creeping closer. Eli breaks past the brush of branches, and Tobias makes himself still.

"Hmm... Where could Tobias be?" Eli calls, playfully looking around.

Tobias grins.

Alora pounces.

"Ahhh!" Tobias screams, scurrying from his hiding place. He loses his balance and tumbles into the stream.

Eli and Alora howl with laughter.

"That's not funny!" he yells.

Lunging for his sister, he knocks her to the ground. Pounding and swiping at her face, she blocks him.

"Enough!" Eli's commanding cry reverberates through the air as he pulls Tobias away from Alora. His sister bares her teeth in frustration, desperately reaching out to him, but Eli blocks her movement.

"You are not to lay a hand on each other. Understood?" he orders.

Growling and scowling, his children oblige and stay in their respective corners. But they only remain silent for a moment.

Tobias shouts, "It's her fault!"

"You should have trained better!" Alora yells back.

"Tricking is not part of the game."

"You would die in battle!"

"Alora," Eli scolds. "Enough, from both of you."

His children go silent under their father's roar. However, both offer a final glaring eye signaling that neither has given in to the other's insults.

"Tobias, gather those fallen branches. Alora, use your abilities and create a fire," he guides.

Not wanting to further anger their father, they follow his instruction.

Eli rests against the tree trunk, watching as Tobias brings the branches and makes the pile. When he completes his task, Alora waves her hands over the twigs. Fire sparks, and the wood ignites, casting warmth over them.

"Well done," Eli praises, brightening their faces. "Tobias, take your wet shirt and hang it on a branch. We will all hear from your mother if you catch a cold."

Tobias chuckles and follows his father's request. Returning, he mimics his father, who lies on his back and watches the clouds. Alora follows, and they all stare as the clouds shift under the current of the wind.

"Papa," Tobias begins. "Are you strong enough to move the clouds?"

Eli smirks, "No, my son. I can create a mighty wind, but nothing is strong enough to shift nature that way."

"That was a dumb question," Alora shoots back.

Tobias rises to confront his sister when Eli rests his hand on him.

"Enough," he groans. "You both will need to learn to get along."

"Papa!" they say, glaring at each other.

Eli raises a hand, silencing them, "I am not asking that you always like each other, but you always must protect each other. I will soon be gone on a journey. For how long, I do not know. Your mother will rely on both of you for much in my absence. To help her, you two must get along more than you fight."

Alora and Tobias watch as their father gazes at the clouds. His children knew of Eli's choice, they knew ever since Onmai left their doorsteps and their parents arguing fluttered from the crevices of their home. While his children have clung to him ever since his decision to leave, Talia has not uttered a word.

"I don't want you to go," Tobias groans.

Alora keeps her eyes on the clouds. Eli glances over, watching as she tries to keep her gaze from him.

"I know you both will miss me. But you can do much in my absence. That is, if you do not kill each other first."

This gets the children laughing.

"I would definitely win," Alora brags.

"Liar! You couldn't even get me off you just now."

"Oh, yeah?" Alora growls back, holding a fireball.

"Yeah," Tobias presses, sticking his tongue out.

Eli sits up, throwing his hands between them. Alora extinguishes her fire, and Tobias pulls back his tongue.

"You must stop this. Your mother will have much to deal with, and this will not help. Am I understood?"

"Yes," they mumble.

"Good," Eli resumes watching the clouds.

The lapping creek fills the silence. The heat of summer is gentle on their skin as the soft breeze flows, creating the sound of whispering from blades of grass.

"I'll train hard while you're gone. You won't have to worry about us. I'll make sure we're safe," Alora promises.

"I won't pee on the seat while you are gone. Mom hates sitting in pee."

Eli grins, "That's my children. I will have nothing to worry about while I am away."

He longs for this moment to last forever. To remain by their side. But as the clouds move and the Crimson Sun comes into view, he knows peace will end. He will execute his role and do what he has to ensure his family's safety, even if that means spending time apart.

"Come, your shirt will be dry, and your mother will have dinner prepared."

"Do you think she'll make your dinner?" Alora asks.

"Yeah, she hasn't left a lot of food for you since Elder Onmai visited," Tobias taunts as he uses wind to gather water from the stream to extinguish the flame.

Eli winces, "Ow! Must you two attack an old man like me when he is down?"

He grabs his children, hoisting each one under his arms. They squirm, and he holds them tighter.

When the children have had enough of their father's antics, he releases them.

"Race you!" Alora taunts, dashing ahead of Tobias and her father.

"Hey!" Tobias yells.

"Quick, or else you will be the last home," Eli says, dashing ahead.

"Not you, too!" Tobias huffs, charging after them.

Chapter Nineteen

19

The thick oak walls adorned with portraits of valor and victory stir Talia's rage as she thinks of the epic loss she will face if her words cannot reach Sage Onmai.

Tomorrow, Alora celebrates her tenth birthday and marks Eli's departure. Talia has unsuccessfully tried to sway his choice. No longer wishing to reason with a fool, she seeks the one person able to change the outcome.

Sneaking through a secret entrance she learned as a young pupil of the sage, Talia tears through rooms and halls in search of her former mentor.

"I wish to see her!" Talia's voice rings through the Elders' Villa.

Tired of her pursuits, she calls for her again and again, until two of the sage's guards confront her.

Squaring her shoulders, she prepares to face them when Onmai appears.

"It is well. Leave her to me," she commands. The guards, while hesitant, obey the order.

"Onmai," Talia growls.

"Quiet your voice," Onmai demands, leading Talia into a nearby room.

"I will do no such thing. Not until I understand why my husband has been told to abandon our children and me?"

"Talia—"

"Do not comfort me, Onmai. Why did they give Eli this task?" she interrupts.

Sage Onmai settles in a wicker chair. She waves her hand, and flames float to candles in the windowless room. The light brightens the ruby-red rugs and shelves of books. The room is one of many studies in the villa.

Onmai offers Talia a chair, but she refuses, choosing to tower over the sage. Sighing, Onmai looks past Talia's anger and sees her fear, "Talia, look past your fear and understand Aster is dead. Some blame Eli for this misfortune."

"Is it Gaia who speaks such foolishness? They have feuded for years. He would seek any opportunity to punish him."

"I know this is hard, but this is the best option."

Talia shakes feverishly, "We might be dead if he wasn't so brazen. There must be another way."

"He might have stopped the war, but he caused some deaths. There are consequences to that."

"Better some dead than an entire village."

"No life is too small."

"Then the same goes for my husband."

The softness in Onmai's eyes fades, "I allow you much room for error, but heed my words. Correct your tone."

Talia's expression is unyielding, yet she lowers her voice, "Why did you not fight for him?"

Onmai sinks into her chair, feeling the pain glistening through Talia's eyes. She watches as the woman, fierce and tireless, tries to still the pain trembling inside.

"Talia, out of all those I have trained, you are most like a child to me. Know that any action of mine has your best interest in mind."

The sage's words show her affection, yet Talia does not soften.

"And like your child, you expect more from me? Will those be your next words, Wise Sage? Because I do not want to hear it." Talia's throat tightens. Each word becomes harder to speak.

"Talia, you are strong, but I fear this decision will turn you bitter, and your soul is far too sweet for such a fate."

"If you do not want my bitterness, keep my husband from this mission," Talia pleads.

Onmai's words add to the agony flowing through her, "Talia, I will not."

"Why?" she demands.

"Because I championed this decision."

"Did you misspeak? Because I thought you said—"

"I did not misspeak," Onmai gently repeats. "When I pulled Eli from the space between our world and the next, I felt a piece of him leave. I thought it meant nothing. My prayer was that he would return to being whole, but I feel you two are no longer one soul. I fear time in this world will only drive you two further apart."

"So you banish him to preserve our union? Such great wisdom from the almighty knower and seer."

Onmai does not chastise her mocking. She only softens her words.

"Talia, I banish him because if anyone can heal him, it's the Chosen One. Perhaps this distance will also teach you about the loss Eli faces."

Talia averts her gaze, desperately trying to hide her brokenness from Onmai.

"Then there is nothing more to be done. I will not only lose my husband once, but twice. A word of advice for you, Wise Sage. The next time you ponder calling someone back to this realm, leave them dead so their loved ones only need to suffer once."

Talia storms away.

As Onmai's heart sinks, she steps forward. Her eyes trail the ground, heavy by her exchange. As her eyes settle on where Talia stood, she sees the tear-stained ground.

Shedding her own tears, Onmai breathes, "Oh my dear, if you only knew what the stars have written."

CHAPTER TWENTY

20

Tired, worn, and defeated, Talia returns to a home empty of siblings bickering, little ones playing, and a husband grumbling. Entering the threshold, the door slams, rattling the house.

Hands cradling her face, she yells, forcing back the tears desperate to flow. Her hand pushes deeper into her eyes, like dams to a rushing river.

"Talia," Eli whispers.

"Why are you here?" she huffs, turning from Eli standing in the door frame.

The floors creak as Eli steps closer, "I was resting while the children played outside. I awoke when I heard your screaming. What is wrong?"

"Go away," her voice cracks. She keeps herself from him, as she feels the dampness on her cheeks.

"Talia," he calls.

His voice stirs her anger, "Leave me alone, Eli. I will fix this myself."

"Talia, there is nothing to be fixed. I must go."

Unleashing her anger, she turns to him, "Why will you not meet me in the middle?! I lose my mind trying to keep our family together, but you walk away so easily."

"Talia, you are the moon that shifts my tides. My desire is never to hurt you, but I am broken in a way you cannot fix. A part of my soul has left me. A piece of me that your love cannot mend."

Talia's soul aches for her lover and her inability to save him. Her desire for him is like the crash of a wave — cold and sharp; it prickles the skin and causes hairs to rise.

She yearns for her words to mend his brokenness, but they do not rise from her chest. The heaviness of his pain and her lack of skill to weave him back together immobilizes her.

Seeing the lack of passion in his eyes causes her to strike. Turning from him, she drives her fists into the wall. The pain radiates from her knuckles but does not dull the pain in her heart.

"Anger, Talia?" he says. "Can you show one thing when you are hurt? Does it pain you so much to be vulnerable? Perhaps time apart would serve us both and satisfy our desires?"

"Eli, do not say such foolish words. My desire is for my family to be whole."

"Bringing the Chosen One back is the best way to do that."

"At what cost?" she breathes. Each word is more painful than the next. Her body shakes and her legs are unable to hold her. Talia sinks to the floor. "I ache for you, Eli, I do. I wouldn't have laid with you and had four children if I didn't. But this is a fool's errand, and I do not want you to go."

"Onmai says she feels this is the time."

"You know what, Eli? She's said the same thing about the last three that went through the portal. Do you know what they all have in common? They did not return. Would you like to be the fourth and leave our children fatherless?"

"What difference does it make when you've already lost me on the battlefield?" he responds.

Her eyes shift to him. She sees the void where their love once lived.

Eli, seeing her sorrow, speaks, "Talia, there are times I feel the glimmer of life swell within me. But I feel a well of despair in my soul that our moments of peace can not fill. Please understand why I must go."

Unable to stand his presence, Talia rises. Straightening her clothes, and tucking the loose hairs that have fallen from her braid, she looks deep into his eyes, "If you insist on embarking on a suicide mission, do so. But you will not have my blessing."

Walking to the bedroom, Talia passes Eli.

He calls to her, watching as she keeps her tears from him, "So you will not see me depart?"

Her steps cease, and her back remains turned to him, "I intend to celebrate our daughter's birthday tomorrow. I hope to see you there."

She does not slam the door, as her anger urges her to do. Talia merely shuts it.

The sound of the bedroom door closing is as quiet as how Talia shuts off the painful parts of her soul. Walking to the bedroom window, Talia gazes out and glimpses Eli, walking away. Watching his departure increases the depth of her sorrow, leaving her with a bleak realization of what it will feel like when he is gone.

CHAPTER TWENTY-ONE

21

The sun has not yet awoken the earth, and the dew is still damp in the air when Eli rouses Alora.

"Wake up, little warrior. I have something to show you."

Alora rubs sleepiness from her eyes, "What time is it?"

He smirks, "It is early, but I have something for you before I depart."

Alora straightens, "That's today."

He nods, "Quick. Ready yourself and meet me outside. Careful not to wake the rest of the house."

Alora nods. Eli tousles her hair before heading out the door.

Eagerly wanting to please her father, she readily dresses and moves stealthily through the house. When she meets him outside, her shoulders straighten under his proud gaze.

"Come," he instructs, opening a portal to the sandy beach.

The air is icy, and the sea is loud as they step through.

"The tide is coming in," she says, looking out into the darkened waters. The portal fazes away, and the only light comes from the few remaining stars and the moon, slowly fading away.

"We'll be gone by the time the tide comes."

Alora follows her father closer to the edge of the waters. He bends down, settling on a spot, "This is close enough. We will need the breeze cast by the waters shortly."

Putting his lips together, he blows. He waves his hands, shaping the gust and shifting the sand. Each grain shifts and morphs under his power until it creates a tiny figurine.

Alora's eyes fill with wonder, "Is that me?"

Eli's smile widens, "Yes."

Alora watches as each grain settles into place on the girl with flowing hair and fists resting on her hips.

"Now, I will need your help with this gift. I want you to create a fire as hot as you can. Can you do that?"

Beaming with pride, she calls on the power of fire. Alora wraps the sandy figure with her flame.

"Very good. Now try to move the energies faster. That will create a hotter flame," Eli instructs.

Alora nods, as beads of sweat form on her brow. The fire widens and almost singes Eli's sleeve.

"Not bigger, Alora. Faster. Try to feel the smallest of particles. Focus on the energy, not the flame."

"I'll try," she says, trying not to lose control of the blaze. She focuses her attention past the fire and into the energy of what she created. She feels the particles and commands them to increase in motion. As the energy bends to her command, they feel the heat intensify.

"Well done. Hold it a moment longer. Right there. Good. Slowly blow away the flame, and I will use the chill in the air to cool what we have made."

She follows his instruction, revealing a glowing figure where the sand once was. As Eli cools the figurine, it becomes more transparent.

filled with amusement, she whispers, "Glass."

He grins, handing her the cooled glass figurine, "Yes, that is how you make glass."

Alora rubs her fingers over the figurine, feeling the last of the warmth from the fire. She cradles it gentler than she holds her siblings, gentler than anything she has ever possessed.

Eli draws her close, as she holds the tiny image of herself. Wrapping his arms around her, she sinks into his warmth, and they watch the sun peek over the horizon.

"You will grow strong in my absence. Of that, I am sure."

Her fingers tighten around her father.

"Will you watch over your mother for me? She is strong, but she gets tired too. Even if she won't admit it."

Alora nods, turning her face closer to him. She breathes deeply, holding on to the memory of his scent, musky and strong, like the scent of her flames.

They watch as the sun reaches higher, casting a bluish hue on the earth. Eli shifts, and Alora reluctantly detaches from him.

"Well then, let's get you home."

"You're not coming?" she gnaws on her lip as the crack in her voice frightens her.

If Eli notices, he says nothing. He merely smiles and waves his hand, opening the portal. As the energies fuse, he forces it wider.

"No, Little Warrior, I am not coming with you. I must go to Onmai and prepare for my departure. And your mother will not wish to see me today."

Plagued by the fear that this was her last time with her father, she runs to him. Wrapping him tightly, she squeezes him. She wants to tell him she'll never let go, but sobs choke her words.

Eli embraces her, tenderly kissing the top of her head as he holds her trembling body until it stills.

"Shed your tears now, if you must. When you walk through that portal, you will be a warrior in training. This is your first mission, and I will have no tears from you while on duty. Understood?"

With one last squeeze, she and the tiny figurine separate from her father. Dry-eyed, she steps through the portal.

Turning to her father, she says, "Will we see you at the portal?"

"That, Little Warrior, depends on your Mother. Be well, Alora. I will see you upon my return."

She waves, watching as the portal fazes out the image of her father. With her chest tight, she is afraid to move, fearing it will cause her tears to fall. Determined to succeed at her mission, she wills herself not to cry.

Lifting her head, she says, "I won't cry. A warrior doesn't cry, and I am a warrior."

Squaring her shoulders, she heads toward her mission and away from childish things.

CHAPTER TWENTY-TWO

22

Onmai strides along the path, her feet stirring through a blanket of red leaves that flutter from the trees like offerings. The birds chirp like melodic harps flying through the sky. The earth is full of hope and excitement, even as loss draws near.

"Did you enjoy your last meal?" Onmai says, greeting Eli.

She loops her arms through his, which Eli gladly takes. Her touch is like a mother guiding a child. Gentle and firm.

"The meal was fine. But I hope it is not my last."

"It will be your last in this world. The spirits only know what food the other world offers," she says as they stroll to her study.

Their words pause when greeted by those wishing to pay respects. Onmai speaks with each pupil and mentor, as if time has no end.

They pass deeper into the villa, surrounded by training dorms and nature. Animals graze undisturbed, reminding all that we are one. As they approach the Elders' Villa, the towering oak tree, Eli rests on his heels, trying to take in all of its massiveness.

"When did the ancestors build this sanctuary?"

"Many, many moons ago, Eli. Long before you or I were even a thought, come, I wish to show you the view from the top."

Onmai leads Eli up the stairs and through the vast corridors, tenderly patting his arm. The sage muses on the transformation that has taken place in recent weeks.

"It's amazing how much time can change things," she reflects. "Just a few weeks ago, you were laid up here in this very same place, beaten and battered. Now look at you — strong and ready for any journey."

Eli maintains his silence as he follows her, reflecting on his separation from those he loves. He once felt so close, but now he departs at a time when they feel far from him.

They reach their destination, a room filled with books and papers. The glint of light shines from the balcony doors, casting a rainbow on the floors.

"Do not mind the mess. I was going over our history and notes from past sages. Sometimes the past holds much wisdom, but other times we must look toward the future."

Onmai strolls to the glass doors leading to the balcony. As she opens the doors, a burst of air washes over the room, ruffling papers held down by makeshift weights.

"Come, take a seat," she says, beckoning for Eli to join her.

Eli follows and settles into the chair that is almost too small for him. As he leans into the back of the seat, its firmness comforts him, like the arm Onmai used to guide him.

Leaning deeper into his seat, Eli observes the clouds floating almost close enough to touch. The warmth of the sun heats his skin as the breeze and subtle scent of rain in the air attempt to rock him to sleep.

"Eli," Onmai calls. "Speak honestly. Do you desire to leave?"

Looking deep into her eyes, Eli assesses her. He sees her depth, her strength, and her desire for truth. He also sees the weariness caused by battle and pain.

"Onmai, I speak honestly when I say I have not been sure of much in the last weeks. But this I am sure of. I did not have rest until you told me I must go. I have no desire to leave my family, but I do not wish to be a shell of myself."

Her eyes linger before turning her gaze over the realm she commands, "Does Talia share your sentiment?"

Eli laughs, "We both know she does not."

Onmai blinks hard, then gives Eli a side-eye, "Does her anger run as hot as it did yesterday?"

"At the same degree."

A bird perches on the ledge, halting their words. They watch it hop closer until it lands on Eli's knee.

"Hmm... That is a good omen. Don't you agree?"

Eli shifts, and the bird flutters away.

"I am not the seer of visions, Wise Sage. But I hope it means Talia will see me off."

"Do you think her anger will keep her from you?"

"Perhaps. Perhaps, not."

They hold each other's gaze until the rise of beating drums fills the air.

"It is time. Are you ready?" Onmai asks.

"Does it matter?"

She laughs, "No, but I thought I'd ask."

Onmai's laughter is loud, like the beating drums that welcome her to the stage and Eli to the portal grounds.

CHAPTER TWENTY-THREE

23

Eli stands before a crowd whose chants shake the ground. He cast his gaze on Onmai, taking her place on a stage above the crowd. Behind her stand the Elders; Gaia, Fin, and Navi. The hollowness of their expressions, void of emotion and empathy, offers no comfort, only judgment. Turning his sights to the crowd, he searches but does not find who he seeks. Seeing none he loves makes the pack on his shoulder heavier.

He searches the crowd, beaming with pride and admiration; they fail to stir excitement within him. The cheering and laughter do not mask the silence of the past days between him and Talia. He longs for her voice or the scent of her body close and warm as opposed to the grassy scent lingering in the air. Eli's lip twitches as the desire to shout out for her grows. His mind begs him to seek what is ahead, yet his body desires for the past. For a time when danger was only a memory, not an ever-present reminder experienced with every shadow or noise.

Above him, Elder Fin hobbles forward, "Sage Onmai, it is time."

Onmai looks into the crowd, searching for Talia, but does not see the tangles of her curls, nor the trail of children that follows her. She places a fist to her stomach, trying to soothe the unease stirring inside, yet with each growing moment the feeling becomes like a knot twisting tighter.

Fin and Onmai hear Elder Gaia clearing his throat above the crowd, "Wise Sage, we can wait no longer."

She cuts her eyes to him, yet her disdain does not wipe the glee from his lips.

Releasing a sigh, she submits to what must be done. Elder Fin returns to his place. Knowing her tone can shift the tide, she places a smile upon her lips, and allows hoy to fill her eyes as she begins the ritual.

"Welcome, all of you," her voice echoes off the training halls, silencing the crowd.

Children and adults alike hang on her every word. Resting her eyes on Eli, she continues, "We have been here before. When the stars align, the vision is most clear, and the sage ruler can open a portal to a faraway land. A land with no magic or abilities, but with a person who can bend the elements. This one is called the Chosen One, and they will be our savior from the Crimson Sun's impending battle."

The crowd cheers and chants victory as Onmai continues the prophecy.

"Even though none before have returned, the prophecy is still true. Doubt not the words of old. The great battle is not upon us, but I am sure it is soon to come. When that day is upon us, we will be glad we had faith to believe."

Her words do not stir fear, but a pleasant anticipation that causes the crowd to chant and dance. Their thoughts focused on thoughts of victory and not the pending loss. Her words continue.

"When will we find the Chosen One, you may ask? How will we know he or she is the one? As the prophecy foretells, we will find the Chosen One when the Crimson Sun is ready to eclipse the Rising Sun.

We will find the Chosen One in a time of great despair, when only their strength can drive away the darkness. I believe this is that time."

Onmai's speech concludes, and her hands move like waves. All eyes shift to the base of the Elders' Villa, where sparks fly, and the air becomes dense.

"I pull the particles of this world and the next, fusing them as one. The place you stand and the place only seen in dreams are now one and the same. Take care and be well, Eli, as you embark on this journey."

The wind shifts, and lightning sparks as the portal opens wider, revealing a world outside Zodia.

The chill of the portal seeps into his bones, yet his heart remains steady and his body still. His soul, however, aches in dread, knowing that he may leave without a last glimpse of his beloved.

Glancing once more into the deafening crowd, he searches for his partner in war and in love.

He looks beyond the unfamiliar faces, searching for Talia's strong shoulders and the coils of her braids. Eli longs for the softness of her eyes, and the cries of their children. But neither Talia nor his children are present. Eli turns to Onmai, who forces a smile.

She mouths, "I'll tell her you said goodbye."

Like a soldier ready to charge the frontline, he bows, showing his final respects. With this act, he sheds the last of his loneliness as he allows duty to be his guide.

Turning away from the cheering crowd and thoughts of his family, he turns toward the pulsing portal. As he steps closer, the whipping sound of wind and the crack of lightning grow louder. With nothing standing between Eli and the portal, he steps forward into the darkness and to the unknown.

CHAPTER TWENTY-FOUR

24

With one child slipping from her hip and another tripping at her feet, Talia pushes and curses for the crowd to move. Tobias and Alora cling close to her as they try not to get lost in the hoard of gatherers. Talia pushes harder, but the crowd knocks her further away as cries of laughter turn to jumping and cheering.

Edging forward, she can see the tip of the portal as it opens. Her heart skips faster, and her legs quake, fearing she will be too late. She steps forward, pulling her children along the way.

Sage Onmai's voice resounds, yet her words are not clear. The crowd grows louder, drowning out the drumming of Talia's heart. Moving closer, the portal becomes clearer, but Eli is not in sight. Her heart twists in agony as thoughts of missing him fill her mind, but hope pushes her forward.

Talia's gaze stays trained on the portal, watching as its light flickers and intensifies to a blinding white. She wills herself not to turn her sights away, though the brightness is overwhelming. The light becomes unbearable. Her eyes drop to her toes, which are battered and bloody from being trampled by the surging crowd. The physical agony does not hold a candle to the aching anguish deep within her soul. The pain only worsens when her eyes return to the portal, and she sees its glow fading in front of her.

"No," she cries, legs weakening beneath her.

"Mama, what's wrong?" Alora whimpers.

"Nothing," Talia snips, but even she hears the trembling in her tone.

Pulling them forward, Talia desperately clings to the hope that Eli has stayed. She prays to the ancestors that he is unable and unwilling to leave their side. Yet, the vanishing crowd brings with it a painful realization; her beloved is nowhere in sight.

Despair brings her to her knees.

The crowd thins, allowing Onmai's eyes to lock on Talia, falling to her knees. The burn of hot tears stings her nose as she leaves the stage and runs to Talia's side. As Onmai approaches, her robe kicks dust with each hurried step. Elder Fin hobbles not far behind.

Onmai steadies her breath, allowing her words not to waver, "Oh, my look here, children. I have brought an ancient friend. His name is Elder Fin. And he has some treats hidden for you. Can you all find them before he eats them all?"

Tobias and Ellie scurry to Elder Fin, excited by the promise of candy and a game. Alora keeps her post by her mother, like a sentry on guard.

Onmai gently places a hand on the small of Alora's back, offering a comforting assurance, "Come, child. All will be fine. I will watch over her for now." She leads her away from Talia, who clings to Jane nestled on her hip.

Onmai reaches out to take Jane from her mother, but Talia draws the little one closer, unable to bear the thought of parting from her. Jane wears Eli's training shirt. It pools around the little one, swallowing her tiny frame. She fought and cried, begging to wear it, hoping it would make her father proud. Now Talia clings to the little one, allowing the scent of Eli's earthy body to comfort her.

The sage backs away. Onmai advises Fin to take the other three children out of earshot. He obliges as Onmai brings herself to the ground.

"I know this is hard. But I promise I had you in mind when I chose him. Things will be better between you two when he returns."

"You know nothing other than dreams. Eli is a fool who couldn't wait to see if I would come."

"Talia, you know that isn't so. Had he waited for you any longer, we all would have missed our chance."

"So I must sacrifice my love and my family for the good of everyone else? Is that your advice, Wise Sage? To grin and bear it?"

"You will not hear me today. There is too much hurt. But understand, I believe in Eli and in the love you share."

Talia laughs. The type of laugh that keeps the pain from swallowing you whole. The sound fills the now empty space that once held rejoicing. Life continues amidst Talia's crumbling soul.

"You believe in our love? A love that couldn't make him whole. Tell me, Onmai, do you know what it feels like to mourn the living? Tell me, will our love solve that?"

Sorrow takes the light from Onmai's eyes and causes her body to tremble. She turns away from Talia as she tries not to absorb the enormity of her pain. As Onmai looks at the place where the portal once stood, she calls to the ancestors, willing a vision to come. She searches for ways to ease the pain but finds nothing other than the void where hope once lived.

The unfamiliar world has harsh wind and dense air that causes Eli's nose to wrinkle. Treetops loom above him, but they are smaller than the ones in his home world. The snowcapped mountains in front of him send a cold chill that aches his bones.

As his eyes adjust to the dimness of this world, he yearns for the brightness of the portal and the image of home. But all hope of returning is gone until he finds the Chosen One and the stars once again align.

Darkness surrounds him as he grapples with no longer feeling the warmth of his children and the ease of Talia at his side.

Turning to the emptiness left behind by the portal, he speaks words that his beloved will never hear, "Our love was not greater than your anger, dear heart."

A sharp cry of an owl overhead startles Eli. He draws his blade. With his palms sweaty around the weapon, he says, "Get a hold of yourself, Eli. It is only a bird."

Shaking away the threat of danger, he returns it to his sheath. Adjusting his pack and steadying his soul, he sets off in pursuit of the Chosen One and the promise of returning home.

II

Part Two

CHAPTER TWENTY-FIVE

25

"She told you what you needed to hear." The words burn, like salt to a wound.

She tries to pull away from the memory, but it pulls her deeper. The hardened floor and unstable chair mean nothing as the sounds in her head take over. The voice, her brother, is more aggressive than her defiant stare. She was a child then, but even now, the memory of his raspy voice makes her feel small.

"Tabatha, you think you can do big things, but you can't!"

Flashes of teasing children peaking through the metal fence and adults crowded around with disdain fill her mind. The children's snickering laughter and adults pointing remind her, she has no voice.

"You should have come to me. You should have let me fix it. Tabatha, look at me when I'm talking to you."

The child version of herself standing in the memory keeps her eyes down, focused on her knee, bruised, and bloody from the playground scuffle. She tried to defend herself, but the attempt ended in ruin. That haunts her now, sealing her lips from protesting.

"You are small. You are a girl. Your role is to marry and live a quiet life. You can't do whatever you want. Mother lied!"

Even now, over ten years after that moment, Tabatha feels the weight of his betrayal, speaking of their mother in that way.

"Don't say her name, Daniel!" Her voice is full and strong, not meek and quiet as she is now.

"Don't say her name." She demands. "You haven't said it since she died. Don't say her name."

The jingle of her mother's bracelet, threatening to slip from her wrists, rings as it does now on her shaking arm.

"Mother believed in a world where anything is possible. She was a liar that should have never taught you that."

"Mother said I am powerful. She told me I can do magical things."

Now a woman on the precipice of change, Tabatha watches her younger self fight to hold on to the power her mother instilled in her. But she feels the glimmer of it slipping away.

"I will apologize for your behavior. Tabatha, your twelfth birthday is soon. You are not to be outspoken, will not be loud, and can not fight. If you act appropriately, it might be enough to save your reputation and mine."

Tears fall as she submits to her brother's scolding. Sitting in the chair of a jewelry shop, Tabatha searches for the resistance that she left on the playground with her tears.

"Tabatha?"

Her doe eyes focus on her fiancé as his docile tone pulls her away from her thoughts.

"Are you okay?" He says, reaching for her fingers.

Tabatha pulls away, wiping her sweaty palms on her jeans. Forcing a smile, she looks from him to the jeweler sitting across the glass counter. The jeweler's watchful eyes assess her and her fiancé, causing heat to rise to her cheeks.

Tabatha runs her fingers through her curls, pushing them from her face. "I'm fine, Sam. I just... I don't know, just drifted."

The jeweler twirls his fingers on the end of his salt-and-pepper mustache. "Ring shopping can be stressful. Perhaps you both can pick out the bands another time."

Moving the bands back into place, locked behind the cabinet, the turn of the lock is enough to force Sam from his seat. As he passes her, she glimpses his balled fists.

Tabatha's fingers press against the silver charms of her mother's bracelet. She finds the same comfort she did as a child, holding the tiny moons and stars.

When her eyes meet the jeweler, Tabatha shrugs. The jeweler plays with his mustache while she gathers her purse. Shuffling out the door, Tabatha approaches Sam, tense and brooding on the street corner.

Tabatha sees the vein pulsing in Sam's forehead. Her lips move faster than her reasoning. "I know you're mad. Your forehead is veiny and red."

Resisting the urge to slap her own forehead, she nibbles her lip. Sam has told her about his light skin, a curse from his enslaved ancestors. Unlike her complexion, which hides her constant embarrassment, his skin makes him feel exposed.

His words slowly seep through his gritted teeth. "You always say the wrong thing, Tabatha. Can you do anything right?"

"I'm sorry."

He continues. "You are always in another world. For once, be a normal person."

His words cause her head to sink lower as she watches the bustling feet move past, uninterested in their fight. Tabatha considers if the passing cars glance their way, but the intrigue isn't enough to draw her eyes from Sam's advancing feet.

"I embarrassed you. I'm sorry," she whispers.

"Tabatha, if your brother wasn't a good friend, I don't know if I would even marry you."

"You mean you wouldn't marry me if my family's restaurant wasn't in a prime location surrounded by gentrification?"

Keeping her arms to her side, she bites the inside of her gum. Her eyes drift from his polished loafer to his clenched jaw.

She watches him control his breathing, but the vein above his eye jumps. "I shouldn't have said that. I love you, but you embarrass me when you're weird."

"So you are embarrassed ninety-eight percent of the time?"

The metallic taste of blood fills her mouth as her teeth bite harder. She winces, frustrated by yet another mistake she has made.

Sam presses his palms into his temples and abandons her on the street corner. Tabatha's fingers find the tiny charms and memories of easier times.

CHAPTER TWENTY-SIX

26

After a bus ride and three blocks, Tabatha can shed the chaos of ring shopping. Amongst the ever changing cityscape is a place that has remained the same her whole life, Hope's Diner.

The diner is more than a place. It's her safe space. It's the place that makes her smile linger even on the worst of days. A haven that still smells of her mother, warm and savory like her soups and pot roast. The essence of her mother still lingers in the broken walls, chipped counters, and fading customers.

Opting to enter from the side door, Tabatha skips passed the entrance, evading the jingle of the front door. Instead, she maneuvers down the alley to the rusted side door. Grabbing her apron from the hook, she ties it around her and fashions her curls into a bun. Pushing away a few loose coils from her face, Tabatha moves deeper into the kitchen to where her brother hovers over documents in his office.

Curled in the doorway against the cold metal frame, Tabatha knows this was why she opted to enter from the side door. Daniel, her brother, flips from one document to the next with a pencil cradled in the crook of his ear. Tabatha does not hide her smile that forms as she watches Daniel scribble notes and scratch out debts. It is the same way their father used to do before he left.

Tapping on the metal frame, Tabatha draws Daniel from his task.

"You look like Dad," she says, sitting opposite Daniel and the pile of papers.

"I don't know if that's a good thing," Daniel grumbles.

Her grin widens, and Tabatha leans forward as she playfully teases her brother. "It's a good thing, for sure. Even if that means you're going to go grey in a few years."

Daniel doesn't smile, nor does he look up from the list of numbers on the page.

"Dad," he begins. "Was irresponsible. He couldn't be man enough to stay when Mom got sick. I'm not him."

Tabatha shifts her eyes from him as the rush of fire warms her cheeks. She, once again, has said the wrong thing. Returning her gaze to Daniel, she scoots to the edge of her chair and peers at his papers.

"What you got there? Looking to the horoscopes to predict dinner service?" She says, taking the newspaper from his desk.

"Look, here's mine. It says, 'Surprising developments in your life might bring a lot of visitors and much adventure.' What did yours say?"

Daniel puts down the paper in his hand. His eyes look annoyed, and she watches him exhale slowly and silently. "I was looking at the business side. Business predicts the cost of produce is rising. Which means I'll have to cut back on supplies or raise prices. Neither will be ideal as we rebrand."

"It will be fine, Daniel. We have figured it out this far. And tonight's special service is sure to generate new business."

Tabatha offers Daniel a soft smile that does not crack the hardness of his eyes.

As he shifts his view back to the documents on his table, Tabatha rolls her eyes and fights the urge to stick her tongue at him.

Instead, she says. "I saw the menu posted on the door. I can make the soups and prep the main courses. Anything else you need?"

"Just get things started. I want you in front of the house."

Rising, she starts for the door. "Are you nervous about the big-time reviewer coming today?"

"We need this to go well, Tabatha. Sam set up this meeting. You only get one shot with opportunities like this."

Grabbing a pot from the shelf, Tabatha is grateful Daniel is out of earshot. As the stockpot fills with rushing water, Tabatha releases an audible groan.

Bringing the pot to the stove, she sets it down harder than expected, splashing water on herself and the stove. Taking a towel, she wipes the water as Daniel's words distract her.

"When were you going to tell me ring shopping wasn't a success?"

Tabatha turns to Daniel, who has emerged from his office. The hanging ladles block her view, but that doesn't stop her from feeling the full intensity of his scowl.

"Tabatha?"

"Daniel."

She hears him sigh, and she turns away, watching as the bubbles form in the pot.

"Tabatha."

She hears the clack of the ladles knocking against each other as he approaches. Her hand grips the damp center of the towel as her knuckles rub against the dry edges. His words are gentle, but she hears the disappointment beneath his words.

"Tabatha, every girl dreams of their parents being there on her big day. Mom is dead, and Dad might as well be. I get why you've been different since the engagement. But don't let fear stop you from marrying the man of your dreams."

"It's not my dream. It's yours!"

Tabatha turns to him and her hands grip her lips. Daniel looks from her to her fingers pressed against her mouth, bare of a ring.

"I know you think I'm being harsh, but it's my job to look after you. That includes making sure you don't ruin your life. Your destiny."

"I hate him," she breathes. "He's mean and rude. He always wants to change me."

The sounds of passing traffic hum in the background easing the silence. The heat rises from Tabatha's cheeks to a burning sensation in her eyes.

"He's not the best, but he's not the worst. Tabatha, you are 26 with no prospects for marriage. I won't always be here to keep you safe. Sam can provide for you and secure the future of the restaurant. Mom's restaurant. You are the only thing stopping us."

"So now I am to be sold off like cattle?"

"No. You are to make decisions like a grown woman."

"What does that mean?"

"It means you want a life where you chase dragons. We don't live in that world, your world. If you stay in that daydream, you'll miss out on reality."

Bruised by his words, she tries to speak confidently. "I don't need a husband or any man to save me. I can be independent."

Daniel shakes his head. "Then put out the fire."

Confused, she turns to where Daniel is pointing. The towel, left too close to the flame, burns. Smoke rises, causing the smoke detector to beep. Tabatha tries to reach for the damp portion of the towel, but her arm gets caught in the flame.

"Ow!" She pulls away, and Daniel comes beside her with a cup of flour.

Pouring the contents into the flame, it dies.

"I could have handled that if you gave me the chance."

"Tabatha, I don't want to argue," he says, looking more tired than when this conversation began. "Sam is a successful man. He's a good match for you. He only wants to change you so you can be better. Mom would like him."

Tabatha flinches. It angers her when he uses their mother to push her in a direction. Turning away from Daniel, she looks at her arm. The fire did not scorch her skin, but it warmed her arm, a cautious reminder she went too close to the flame.

Daniel takes her arm and pours a thin layer of honey. "As you grow older and wiser, you'll realize I was right. Look around, Tabatha. Don't make the same mistake as those other businesses who blindly refused to accept the truth. They failed to take advantage of the opportunity and are now left behind. See the change that is coming and make the right choice. "

She meets his gaze. "So I'm an investment opportunity?"

Daniel drops her hand. Putting the honey back in place, he walks to his office. Before he slams the door, he turns to offer her one last phrase. "Tabatha, I want you to invest in yourself."

The door slams, rocking the ladles that clatter frantically. When the rocking settles, she is grateful for the silence. Tabatha takes the last of the burned cloth and deposits it into the trash. Sweeping the flour from the floor, she looks at Daniel's door.

Thinking of the horoscope and its prediction, she frowns. "If this is how my adventure starts, I'd hate to see how it ends."

Chapter Twenty-Seven

27

Tabatha's finger drums on the linoleum counter, adding to the boisterous passengers disembarking busses. There muffled sounds and quick steps sounding like the quick beats of her heart as she waits for the restaurant reviewer.

Each crack of the door brings with it the hiss of brakes, car horns, and the passing sigh as Tabatha exhales her held breath.

Clasping her charms, she tries to slow her breathing, which is only quickened when the waitstaff startles her. "Has he come yet?"

Tabatha turns to the woman. She's a new face. The woman looks older than her and is not interested in continuing a long conversation. Tabatha shakes her head 'No.'

Looking at Tabatha a moment more, the woman raises her brow. "You think you'll be able to tell who this reviewer is?"

Tabatha shrugs, hoping she will notice. A table waves and the waitstaff leaves her side to tend to them. The door swings open, filling the diner with the sounds of a bustling city evening and more patrons.

Tabatha seats familiar locals, and some new customers brought in by the announcement of a fresh menu. Following a crowd of patrons is a lone man carrying a briefcase. His tailored jacket and the glint of a fancy watch make him look out of place.

After seating the man, Tabatha moves to lock eyes with the staff member. Smiling, she signals about the reviewer being present.

Not adding a smile to her face, the woman shifts her attention and provides him with prompt service. Breathing deeply, Tabatha feels a wave of nostalgia wash over her as the familiar rhythm of the diner returns.

"Order up!" Calls the chef in the back, no doubt under scrutiny from her brother.

As plates move in and out and more people enter, it feels like the days and nights Tabatha clung to her mother's leg. She remembers the feeling of being jostled as her mother hobbled from one side of the diner to the next. Their mother tended to customers while yelling at their Father to pick up the pace.

The man with the tailored jacket snaps his fingers, rousing Tabatha from her memory.

"Excuse me?" He calls, emphasizing each syllable.

Looking around, she searches for the waitstaff. Finding the woman engrossed in tending to other tables, Tabatha approaches the man. When she is at his side, he is tapping his pen on a pad beside barely touched plates.

The man doesn't glance her way as he gestures to the dishes.

"Remove this." He snaps, tapping his lips with his napkin.

"Was there something wrong? I can try to fix it." She offers.

"Remove it, I said, and bring me an order of the house mac and cheese."

The man's eyes never leave the menu, as Tabatha stares at the scarcely eaten meal.

Dropping the menu, he glares. "Didn't you understand me?"

"Oh, sorry. I just. Wouldn't you like to eat more or take it home even? I could ask the cooks to change something." Tabatha presses the bracelet's charms, but her racing heart does not ease.

"I said remove it. I will not ask again. Bring me the mac and cheese immediately for this inconvenience."

"I don't mean to be inconvenient." She whispers. "It's just... There are so many hungry people I would hate to waste—"

"Waste!? Bring me your manager. Who are you to lecture me?"

"I didn't mean to lecture you; I'll take it immediately."

Tabatha grabs for the plate, but the man takes hold of it.

"No! Bring me the manager. I want to talk to him about your behavior."

Pleading, Tabatha grips the plate tighter, drawing it to her. "Really, that's unnecessary. I will bring you whatever you want."

"Let go, you vile creature."

"Hey! That's not nice." Tabatha scolds.

Her fingers let go of the dish, slinging gravy onto the man's perfectly pressed shirt. A collective gasp runs through the restaurant as everyone watches in awe, and then an eerie hush overwhelms them, only to be replaced by her throbbing heart.

"I will get someone right away."

Tabatha races away, calling for Daniel, who hovers over the chef.

"Daniel! Don't be mad," she begs, but it is too late.

Moving from his table, the man yells at anyone who will listen to him. His voice echoes off the walls about the poor service. Daniel pushes past Tabatha as she cowers behind the kitchen window.

The chef peers over her shoulder. "Hey, I know that guy; he's a food columnist in the paper."

Tabatha groans, and the cook scurries back to his position. Tears form as she clutches her bracelet. Subjected to public humiliation,

Daniel stands in the diner, full of eyes glued upon him. When he diverts his attention to Tabatha cowering in the kitchen, her heart sinks. Yet another glare of disappointment and another impending lecture to endure. But this time, the stare is more seething. It is the same glare she endured as a child standing with skinned knees and shattered confidence.

CHAPTER TWENTY-EIGHT

28

Her feet drag across the pavement as both her body and mind feel heavy. Light glimmers from buildings like stars, as night causes a chill in the air. However, the night breeze isn't the only thing sending a shiver through her bones.

She stops. Tabatha forces the tears not to fall as she recalls the quiver as her brother spoke. She felt him hot with anger as he uttered one word.

"Leave."

The way he spoke paralyzed her, not because of the coldness, but from the way he kept his eyes from her. She was more than a disappointment. It was like he wished she no longer existed.

Squeezing her eyes closed, she stops the tears that try to break free. The buzz from her phone pushes the image away. She searches her bag but can not find the device.

"Where is it?"

Combing through her bag, Tabatha reaches for the glow of the screen. Before her fingers can wrap themselves around the device, someone yanks her purse from her shoulder.

"Hey!" she yells, gripping the bag.

She pulls it closer, and an orange hat-wearing teen jerks it back.

"Give it to me, hoe," he yells, pulling harder.

"Don't call me that!" she shouts, holding it tighter.

She desperately searches for someone to come to her aid, but no one glances her way. Tabatha is alone in a land of people scrolling their phones and focusing on their troubles.

Her hope strengthens when she locks eyes with a green hat young man approaching them.

"Help me, please!" Tabatha begs, as she feels her fingers shaking and her grip loosening.

He smiles at her, and her lips stop trembling. Too focused on his reassuring expression, she didn't see the fist coming toward her. Tabatha cries out as the pain in her temple radiates across her face.

She stumbles back, and Orange Hat pulls the bag from her. When the black specks and bile stirring settle, she watches them run into the park.

Furious and determined not to lose anymore this day, she dashes after them.

Deeper into the park they go with Tabatha on their heels. The hat-wearing thieves dip behind a thick brush of bushes to investigate the contents of her bag. The duo prepares to look inside when they hear beating feet against the ground.

"Give it back," she shouts.

They dart from the bushes, running deeper into the park. Her nose flares as her lungs burn for more air, but she pushes after.

Orange and Green Hat run until a construction zone blocks their path. When they turn, Tabatha inches closer, cutting off their way to the street.

Breathless, Tabatha extends her hand for her purse.

Orange Hat is holding it, but Green Hat gestures for him to give it back.

Orange Hat steps forward, "Sorry, miss. We didn't mean any harm."

"Thank you. You can get hurt taking things. If you need food, I work at a diner. I—."

Startled, she stops. Orange Hat extends the bag to Tabatha, then pulls it back, throwing it at Green Hat, who moves behind her.

Locked in a game of monkeys in the middle, Tabatha runs back and forth. The boys snicker, waiting for her to approach, only to pass it back to the other side.

Wearily, her legs quiver. Her movements slow until she can move no more. Tabatha's body shakes, and she weeps. Her cries flow like rivers, refusing to be held. Angrily, she swipes her face, but she is powerless even against her tears.

Her body stills when she feels the lightness of a finger on her wrist. Clearing her eyes, she sees Green Hat. Holding her purse in one hand, his free hand brushes her wrist. Meeting her eyes, he smiles.

His smile turns sinister as he rips Tabatha's bracelet from her wrist.

"No!" she shrieks, a shrilling sound that scatters roosting pigeons. The boys take off toward the street.

Refusing to lose the last symbol of her mother's affection, Tabatha runs, pushing past the burning in her thighs. She runs, ignoring the pulsing in her head. Running like she wants to escape everything that is chasing her, she pushes forward. Faced with the intersection, she sprints faster, unwilling to lose the pair in the hustle of crossing traffic. But she is too far behind.

Cars pass. The light turns red.

Orange Hat crosses the intersection and waits for his friend to follow.

The light turns, and cars start down the street.

Green Hat follows behind, but he can not hold his pants up while holding her bracelet and Tabatha's bag. He trips and falls, both spilling the contents of her purse, bracelet, and becoming caught in traffic.

Green Hat lies in the path of an oncoming truck barreling down the street. Its horn blares, warning him to move from his path. The truck is too fast. The brakes squeal, but it will not stop in time.

Caught in the glow of the bright lights, Green Hat is too frightened to move. Tabatha is upon the crosswalk but will be a causality herself if she steps forward. Staring at the truck speeding forward, and Green Hat caught in the path, she reaches toward him.

"No!" she shouts.

With all her might, she wills the boy to be blown from danger. She squeezes her eyes shut to slow the dizziness that comes with her next breath. Stumbling to the ground, she grips her head to steady herself and avoid the pop of crushing bones. But no screams or cracks follow. When she opens her eyes, the horrific scene she expected is not within her sights. She stares at Green Hat, looking at her wide-eyed and out of the path of the passing truck. Tabatha searches for who has pulled the boy to safety, but no one has stirred from their paths. The boy staggers from the crosswalk and down the street with his friend. The beeping of the walk sign signals it's time to pass. Tabatha runs to retrieve her items. When she finds her mother's bracelet, she whimpers, "No. Oh, no."

Caught in the truck's path, her mother's bracelet lies shattered. The truck crushed the tiny charms and chain. "Mom..." she sobs, staring at the fragmented pieces of the reminder of her mother. Trying to salvage what's left, she inches forward but jumps back when the horns blare, and cursing drivers urge her to move.

Removing herself from the crosswalk, she watches as the last of her beloved trinket becomes more broken and scattered. With no more tears left to give, she turns to find her way home when a large bearded man blocks her path.

"Did you see that? Did you see what you did?" the man's eyes are wild and frantic. His dirt-caked hands grasp her shoulders, shaking her.

"Stop! Don't touch me," she shrieks.

"Did you see?" he presses.

"See what?"

"You," his voice, like his eyes, is full of intensity.

Tabatha tries to pull away from the crazed man, but his grip is powerful.

"I..me..?"

"You pushed that boy. You. I saw you create a blast so strong it pushed him forward. I have been searching for you, Chosen One."

Horrified, Tabatha thrusts her hands forward, pushing the man from her. She runs for as long as she can. She runs until her lungs refuse to fill with air. Braced against a building. Her breath slows, and her world spins less. Looking around, she searches but finds no one.

The bearded man is gone. But even though he is out of sight, she can not outrun his words: "Chosen One."

Why on earth would she be that?

CHAPTER TWENTY-NINE

29

Finding Sam's key is usually the delay that keeps Tabatha in the hallway, but tonight her shaky hands try to maneuver the key to the doorknob. Hearing the announcer come over the TV, she knows Sam is completing his nightly ritual of watching the game. He loves it. He loves it more than hearing about her day, or tending to any minor inconvenience. So she knows he won't come to the door for her.

The key is in the lock, Sam's lock, and she turns it. Stepping inside, she sees the house messy and waiting for her attention. Tabatha had emptied the sink that morning, but the dishes are now piled high.

Tabatha searches for the hook to place her coat, but it's not there. This is not her home. The move happened recently, perfectly timed with the departure of Sam's housekeeper. She was resistant to it, but everyone told her the move would be wise.

The keys and flattened purse hardly touch the counter before Sam scolds Tabatha, "Where have you been? I called you twenty times."

He keeps his back to her. His attention focused on the game. Tonight it's football. Tabatha stares, wondering if he saw her, would he move his feet from the table? Would he come to her aid if he saw the lack of luster in her eyes? Is there anything about her that would take his eyes off his prized possession?

Reaching for the comfort of her charms, she shudders when her fingers do not find the curve of the moon or the chip on the star's surface. She longs for the sound of them clicking together or for the sensation of her hands warming the cool metal.

"My phone has been ringing nonstop from your brother, my food friend, and everyone else who heard about tonight's disaster. How can one person make such a mess?"

With no room left to fight, she focuses her attention on a pizza box. Flipping the lid, she sighs. Defeated. The box is as empty as she is.

"Why aren't you answering me?" he asks, finally turning to her.

Moving the pizza box to the trash, she shrugs. Her words, if she could find them, wouldn't matter. Not to him. She has no energy to be blamed for her failures and no desire to be reminded of the consequences of her actions.

"Tabatha, you're filthy. What have you been doing?"

His tone is absent of concern, but judgement is present. It fills the room until even the announcer recounting a play seems judgmental. Her shoulders rise and fall. The night's events replay in her mind. Sharing them with Sam would mean being hurt again.

Looking at her dirty hands, she shuffles toward the bathroom when Sam steps in her path.

He towers over her, reminding her she is powerless. Sam has a knack for that. Reminding everyone how small they are and how big his money is. Tabatha looks into his face, marked with frustration. She sees how deep his brows are drawn together and the wrinkle in his nose. He's not ring shop mad, but his reddening neck shows he is getting there.

"Tabatha, tonight wasn't just about you. Do you know how many favors I had to call in to get my friend to review your brother's restaurant? I look like an idiot. How can you be so selfish?"

Sam's jaw grows more rigid with each word, but she can feel herself staring blankly. She is unafraid of his anger, nor shaken by his disappointment. But she is angry. A feeling that hasn't been present for a long time. It's not a rage that shows like Sam's, but something that burns within.

The crazed man's words ring in her ears: *I saw you.*

Has Sam ever seen her? Seen beyond her screw-ups? Has anyone?

"Tabatha, do not zone out. I deserve answers. Say something!"

"Say something," she repeats. It's robotic. Like a confirmation of what he wants because she fears if she says something, she will not stop.

"Say something," he commands. The words are pressured and thin, like his patience.

She feels her lip tremble and her heart race faster as the fire burning inside longs to be heard. To be anything other than silent.

"I am not selfish. I am kind, a good friend, I'm loving," her hands move to her mouth, silencing her words. Hearing the power in them frightens her.

"You are selfish. You messed up our big night. Did you even try not to be yourself? Then you disappear and don't answer my calls. I'm not the bad guy here. You are."

Her hands move from her lips to her side. Dirt from her fingers leave a darkened mark over her lips, a pleading reminder for silence, but the fire does not die. It burns hot as it did when the man spoke his words: *Chosen One.*

Tabatha's eyes meet Sam's, and for the first time, she sees what's behind the anger. Fear.

Tabatha's lips move, but it's like someone else speaks. Like a version of herself that she has kept hidden away takes center stage. When the sound echos to her ears, they feel foreign, yet so right, "You do these things; you choose me, because of what I can do for you. I am an investment. But you don't choose me because you see something special in me. You choose me so you can marry into our mother's restaurant." She doesn't yell. She does not scream. But each word satisfies the fire that burns, that pushes her to choose herself.

Her eyes are fixed on Sam's face, searching for understanding, but the voice of the announcer on the screen distracts his attention away from her.

Sam turns back to her, ending the conversation, "You're not making any sense. I'm done with this conversation."

I see you. The crazed man's words are like flint to the spark.

"No," she says defiantly.

Sam does not turn.

"No," her voice is stronger.

"Give it a rest, Tabatha. In the end, nothing will change. You'll still cause problems that I have to solve. Let me enjoy the game, and I'll figure out how to fix your mistakes tomorrow."

Returning to his position on the couch, his eyes remain on the screen. The fire burns, beckoning her to leave.

Leave. The word beats inside her. The same painful statement her brother spoke to her now becomes her freedom.

With her purse in hand, she reaches for the handle. With her fingers brushing the knob, Tabatha pauses. Not to stay, but to do one more thing. One more act of freedom.

She removes his key.

As the key jingles, Sam never turns from the television. He doesn't ask what she is doing.

Removing it from the key ring, she slides it across the counter. She returns her attention to the door as a player scores. Sam leaps up cheering, as Tabatha walks out the door.

CHAPTER THIRTY

30

S tretching, Tabatha immediately regrets that decision as her body sends a jolt of pain through her. She groans under her body's reminder of the night's events, filled with running, new encounters, and loss.

Turning her cheek to the wall, cooled by the morning air, she rests her pounding head upon it. Morning breeze drifts over her from the cracks in the windowsill. The pain eases, and Tabatha rolls over to look at the old apartment.

This apartment is above the restaurant, a safe place for her family to lie when tending to an overnight roast or fulfilling large catering orders. It had even been a resting place for those in need when their mother was alive. Now, it's just a spare space collecting dust.

As Tabatha lies in the bed, she looks around the old space and sees images of her mother. She sees her in the makeshift kitchen, washing fruit in the sink and taking snacks from the mini-fridge as they wait to taste what was cooking below. She remembers how her mother braided her hair on the old plaid couch. The bathroom with shower and stall was the place she found her mother falling asleep often. This has been a place full of happy memories.

A tear falls from her eye and trickles down her nose. Quickly wiping it away, she turns her attention to the buzzing mini-fridge. Her stomach growls, reminding her she has not eaten since yesterday afternoon. The dust-covered counters do not help her feel optimistic about what she will find in the kitchen.

Turning her body to the coolness once more, she readies herself to go downstairs in search of breakfast.

She stands and lands back on the bed. Grumbling, she runs her fingers over her cheek. The area feels puffy and hard. Tabatha recalls the man's fist coming toward her and turns her attention to the bathroom.

"Okay, one more time," she says, preparing to stand on shaky legs.

This time, she stands slower. She waits for the dizziness to fade and makes her way to the shower.

Reaching the bathroom, Tabatha braces herself against the door as memories flood her. Seeing his hygiene products across the sink reminds her of how Daniel used this space in the days following their mother's death. In those days, Tabatha stayed with a family friend as Daniel tried to juggle running the restaurant and making funeral plans. In those days, Tabatha remembers seeing him in blurs.

Shaking the memories from her head leaves a fresh wave of pounding, like drums. Nauseous with hunger and dizzying pain, Tabatha slowly moves the old products toothbrush, gel, and her brother's old deodorant from the bathroom. Near the sink is a storage cabinet, another homage to her mother. In it is filled with samples if shampoo, toothpaste, and other items her mother would gather from hotels and anyone willing to donate. Reaching into the storage cabinet, Tabatha removes her hygiene items.

Shaking, she bends to the lower shelves filled with towels. She places the items down and remembers the storage closet where her mother kept clothing for those in need.

Stepping out of the bathroom, Tabatha looks beyond the pile of boxes. Just behind them is the closet. As she moves the boxes, Tabatha tries to avoid peering inside at the reminders of their home. Daniel often had to choose between the mortgage or rent for the restaurant. Neither Daniel nor Tabatha wanted to lose another piece of their mother so soon, so the boxes came here and never left following the foreclosure of their family home.

Reaching the closet, Tabatha coughs as a cloud of dust fills her airways. She smiles and finds a dress covered in yellow sunflowers. Satisfied with her find, she returns to the bathroom, where she turns the water on scorching.

Tabatha moans as the warmth soothes her tender shoulders and dulls the throbbing of her sore body. Water flows through her scalp, tightening her coils. When she emerges from the shower, she feels more alive.

Wiping the condensation from the mirror, she grimaces at her reflection. Her face doesn't ache, but the purplish bruising around her temple looks painful. Pulling her curls closer to her face and praying that her curls hold, she promises to get a diffuser.

Her stomach growls.

Looking at her reflection, she makes a plan, "Okay, quick breakfast downstairs. In and out. I'll come back for my shift like nothing's happened."

Her reflection doesn't look confident, but Tabatha pushes that away as another wave of hunger washes over her.

CHAPTER THIRTY-ONE

31

Tiptoeing inside, she flips on the light. Tabatha could have maneuvered around the familiar place in the dark with ease, but the light is a welcome tool to ensure Daniel was not sitting in the dark. Edging forward, her breath eases when the light reveals the empty office chair.

"Why am I hiding from you?" she breathes, as she continues to listen for him shuffling papers. Shaking away her concern, she moves for the fridge. When she looks inside, Tabatha reviews her options.

"Eggs, bread, milk, bacon... French toast sandwich!" She cheers, starting the batter.

Butter glides across the screaming pan, melting away the pains of yesterday. Flowing from pan to ingredient, her sense of safety and security grows, until she hears movement.

"Hello?" she calls.

No response, other than the sizzle of bacon crackling in the oven. Grabbing a mitt, she pulls it and sets the sheet pan atop the stove.

"Crispy!"

Dancing to the smells and sizzle of the pan, Tabatha halts when her eyes catch the dark outline of a figure.

"Who's there?" Tabatha yells, attempting to scare off the figure, but even she hears the tremble in her words.

The shadow comes into view, revealing the man from last night.

Grabbing a spatula, she waves it at the man, "Stay back! How'd you get in here?"

"I have learned how to pick a lock or two while in this world," the man says, stepping into the light.

His clothes look worn, his beard and locs are caked with dirt and debris, but through all of that, she can see a calm in his eyes.

"Step back, I'm warning you. I will use this. A spatula is a deadly utensil."

His cracked lips grin. He moves closer, and Tabatha takes a step back, pressing against the stove.

When he speaks with a hint of an accent, she can not place, "It can be deadly. But not in the manner that you hold it. I can show you how to wield it better in training."

The towering man is within reach of her. Her eyes dart to the exit, but she fears he is close enough to stop her.

Watching her eyes searching for escape, he speaks, "I don't mean to scare you, but I have been searching for you for a long time. I had given up hope until last night. Last night, I remembered the prophecy and its tale of despair. Just like it foretells, I found you during a time of great hardship. Chosen One, you have my word; I will not harm you."

It is still early, and no one will be at the restaurant for another few hours. Tabatha glances at the clock and says, "Someone will be here any minute. When they find you, you'll be in trouble."

Ignoring her words, he continues, "My name is Eli. I am from Zodia, a land in desperate need of you."

Eli inches closer.

"Help! Help!" Tabatha yells.

Running his hands through his locs, he reaches for a knife, silencing Tabatha.

With the knife in hand, he reaches for Tabatha. She tries to recoil away, but he grasps her tighter. Placing the knife in her hands, he closes her fingers around it and moves it to his neck.

Her breath stills.

Eli's words are slow as he urges her to calm, "Please. I will not hurt you. If you need to keep this knife at my throat, then do so, but please listen to my words."

His fingers tighten over her hand, forcing the blade deeper into his skin. Tabatha's eyes widen at the indentation. It does not draw blood, but she is afraid if she flinches, it will harm him.

Stammering, she says, "Okay, fine. I'll listen, but mister, you have this all wrong. No one needs me. Everyone tries to get rid of me."

"You underestimate how special you are. I do not have long to convince you. In the coming weeks, the stars will align, and I will open a portal to my homeland," he says, easing his grip on her.

"Sir, what?"

"Not, sir, Eli. My name is Eli," the man's voice cracks, and a smile widens. "It feels odd to say my name. I can not remember the last time I have said it or heard it, spoken back."

"Okay, Eli. Do you think we can have this conversation a few steps apart?"

Eli nods, releasing her, but leaves the knife in her hands.

She holds it close to her, watching as the man looks past her.

Pointing to the pan behind her, he asks, "Should you tend to that?"

Turning, she takes the once weaponized spatula and removes the bread from the pan. Tabatha frowns at the blackened, yet edible, side of toast. Her stomach growls, followed by the loud roar of the man's belly.

"Um... Are you hungry?"

Eli's eyes brighten as he nods.

Grabbing an *extra* plate, she layers the French toast, bacon, and tomato. Slicing it in half, she places it on the second plate and offers it to Eli. They eat in silence. Tabatha never moves her eyes away, watching as he devours the food in bites.

Clearing her throat, she asks, "Portal?"

Eli wipes his mouth, "Yes, Chosen One. I will explain much over the coming weeks, but I want to see your training. When shall we begin?"

"First, let's start with my name, which is Tabatha. Not Chosen One. Second, what training?"

"I want to see more of what you did last night."

"Last night?"

"The boy. You moved him. The elements are not aligned in this world. Creating such a gust is some feat."

The clock tics, drawing her gaze. Someone will enter soon, and she is not ready to explain why she's with a big bearded man with leaves in his hair.

"Sir... I mean Eli. I don't know what you think you saw. You look like things have been rough. Have you hit your head? Is there family that I can call?"

"I am not wrong!" his words reverberate off the walls, shaking the ladles.

She pulls away, and he lifts a hand to stop her, "I'm sorry. I didn't mean to yell. But I am not wrong. I can't be. Time is running out."

Tabatha watches as the man's eyes become as frantic as the night before. Eli flinches when her hand rests on his.

"Eli, you look really scared. I want to help you, but I don't know how."

Pulling his hand from hers, he rests his face in his hands, "I am not scared, just worn. It has been days since I have rested."

His weariness makes her heartache, and her words spill out before she realizes what she has said, "I know where you can rest for a little."

CHAPTER THIRTY-TWO

32

Leaving Eli in the restaurant apartment, Tabatha purchases some makeup to conceal the bruising and a diffuser. With curls lifted and face less bruised, she returns to the restaurant in time for dinner service. She finds the waitstaff serving tables and the cook in his station.

Her feet take her around the corner to her brother, where Daniel will be in his office reviewing papers. It's a journey that has been part of her routine for years, yet when she sees the flicker of anger in his eyes, she hesitates.

Daniel is not shifting through papers, as he usually is. No, today he is staring at her as he clutches the daily paper. Tabatha's arm hangs, waiting to rap on the door. She opens her mouth, but when Daniel averts his gaze from her, no words come out. She tries again to speak when Daniel stops her.

"Close the door," he says.

Desperately wanting the comfort of her bracelet, she bites down on her lip, distracting herself from her pulsing heart.

As she closes the door, she sees the chef and waitstaff peeking her way. The door shuts, and she takes a moment to steady herself before turning to Daniel.

"Daniel, I just wanted to say—"

"I need you to leave, Tabatha."

She flinches.

Turning to him, she can feel the way her heart tightens with pain as she asks, "Why?"

Her legs feel unsteady. She draws her hands behind her back, afraid he will see them shake.

Daniel stares at her. He slams the paper down, and her eyes flicker to the pages. Tabatha reads the headline, and her eyes grow bigger.

"Daniel, I..." her words trail off as the words become blurred by tears.

"The headline was just the start: *No hope for Hope's Diner*. The gentleman whose shirt you painted with gravy described the food as mediocre and the service, well, you can guess what he wrote about that."

His last words reveal the bite he's been masking. Tabatha grips her bare wrist; the moisture from her palm makes her heart race.

Daniel continues, "I have spent all night trying to reach Sam, but he won't answer. Maybe I can fix this if I can get this man back. But I can't make this right with you here. I need you gone."

Tabatha feels her throat tighten as she looks into his eyes. Eyes that never ask her for anything, yet at this moment, beg for her to leave.

"Leave? For how long?"

"I don't know. Just until I figure this out."

Tabatha's soul fills with anguish as relief eases into her brother's face. She can see how grateful he is to speak these words. As if he has wanted her gone all his life. Was she such a burden to him? The thought makes her nose burn as she keeps the tears from falling.

Daniel pushes away from the desk. Startled, Tabatha tries to speak, but he pushes past her.

"I have to make sure everything is okay. Excuse me," he says, leaving Tabatha in the office.

Daniel leaves the door ajar, and Tabatha can feel the burning gaze of the staff without having to turn around. She stands still, her heart racing as her head pounds relentlessly. Attempting to steady her hands, she takes a deep breath and braces herself for what is to come.

"How can I leave this place, the only home I've got left?" she whimpers to walls that used to hold all the answers.

Gazing out into the kitchen, her brother and staff switch between one task after the other without needing her aid.

No one looking to choose her.

Leaving the office, she searches for the only person who wants her presence: Eli.

CHAPTER THIRTY-THREE

33

Keeping herself from being seen, Tabatha travels upstairs. When she opens the door, her heart beats faster. She finds the apartment empty of the mysterious man. Rooted by the door, lost and alone, she feels herself sinking lower until she hears movements behind the bathroom door.

"Oh, thank goodness," she says, placing her hand on her racing heart.

Eli emerges from the bathroom.

"Eli?" she questions, looking at the man cleansed of dirt and leaves. His hair and beard remain in disarray, though he stands straighter and appears more alert.

"I hope you do not mind, Chosen One. I found some clothing in the back. May I wear them?"

"Of course," she replies as joy returns to her.

Nodding, he moves his old things from the bathroom into the trash bin.

"You are back earlier than expected," he says.

"My schedule is a bit more free for a while."

"Very well. When would you like to train?"

She opens her mouth to protest, but fear stops her. She does not want him to leave. Instead, she places a smile on her face.

"Whenever works for you. I'm game."

Eli smiles, and for the first time, she sees a light in his eyes that makes her warm.

"The day is almost gone. We begin in the morning. For now, Chosen One, ask me anything you would like," Eli says, moving to the couch. Tabatha sits beside him and watches him settle into the softness of the chair, waiting for her to speak.

"Well, okay, um... you said you aren't from here. You are from a different place?"

"Yes, Zodia."

"Zo-what?"

"Zodia. My home world. It is a more balanced world than this."

"What does that mean?" she questions.

"That is not important. What is important is the prophecy and you?"

"Prophecy? Like a horoscope?"

He raises an eyebrow, "I don't know what a horoscope is. The prophecy is a tale told in my world for generations about the eclipse of the Crimson Sun and the Rising Sun. When that happens, war and immense destruction will occur. But you, Chosen One, can end all of that with your power."

Eli pauses. Shifting closer to her, he asks, "Chosen One, have I said something to upset you? You look unwell."

She averts her gaze, trying to steady the swirling room. Anxiety grips her as she considers that she may have let someone into her place who would be more at home in a sanatorium. Daniel's judgment weighs on her mind, and she fears being seen as foolish and a burden for having this man in her presence.

The spiraling thoughts stop when Tabatha feels the warmth of Eli's hand on her wrist. The gentle touch fills her with the ease of her mother's bracelet.

Looking into his eyes, she says, "Eli, I don't have any powers. I'm powerless."

He does not move his hand, "Chosen One, you are powerful. I saw it with my eyes. I have seen much in this world, but nothing like what I see in you."

Even though she believes the words come from a delusional man, she finds comfort in them, in his kindness.

Her dress pocket buzzes, pulling her away from his warmth. When she looks at the screen, she groans. Declining Sam's call, she stuffs her phone back into her pocket.

Eli watches her, and Tabatha looks away, not ready to discuss Sam.

"I'll grab you some blankets for the couch. I'm sure you didn't sleep yet."

Moving from the chair, she grabs the linen and passes it to Eli. Taking the sheets; he spreads them on the floor.

"Eli, you can sleep on the couch. I know you're long, but wouldn't it be softer?"

"This will be fine, Chosen One."

She watches him settle on the floor as if it is as plush as a bed. He keeps his back to the wall of the counter and his eyes fixed on the door. She follows his gaze and turns the deadbolt, hoping to ease his discomfort. Tabatha does not look back at him but settles in her bed.

As she lay staring at the ceiling, her pocket buzzes again. She does not remove it. She only lets it ring until it stops. Below she can hear the back entrance open and shut as someone tosses trash into the bin.

"Eli?"

"Yes?"

"Can you do something for me? Can you call me Tabatha from now on?"

"Very well, Tabatha. I will call you that from now on."

Smiling, she closes her eyes and listens to the hum of the night while Eli rests on the hardened floor. As her mind becomes restful, a thought occurs.

"One more thing."

"Yes, Tabatha?" he grumbles.

Listening to the muffled sound of his voice, filled with fatigue and irritation, draws her smile wider. Subduing her giggle, she asks, "What happens if you're wrong about me?"

"Then all my people and I perish."

CHAPTER THIRTY-FOUR

34

As the sun peeks over the horizon, Tabatha shudders at the chill in the air. She trails behind Eli as they approach a building with broken windows. It's a decommissioned factory on the edge of town, where nothing and no one goes.

Eli kept the clothing he found yesterday, a pair of sweatpants and a dark-colored tee shirt. Tabatha hung up her dress and went for something more practical. She found a pair of jeans and a shirt that she wished had longer sleeves.

Tabatha wraps her arms tighter around herself as they enter the damp-smelling building. She contemplates if her horoscope or her bad choices led her here, surrounded by empty beer cans and dirty walls. The thought fades as a waft of human waste, and cigarettes wrinkle her nose.

Eli walks deeper into the building when a mouse crosses his path. Tabatha's hairs rise, and a scream escapes her lips, while his steps never falter.

"Is there a reason we are in this scary building with mice running around?" she squeals as she almost hops into Eli.

Never turning her way, Eli marches forward, "Mice will be the least of your worries on the battlefield."

Tabatha glares at the back of his head but quickens her steps.

"Morning is a good time to train. Those who sleep in this building migrate away, while those that remain offer no disturbance. We will need few interruptions if you are to be battle ready."

"I'm the Chosen One; don't I come battle ready?"

Eli turns to her, and she steps back, fearing the sarcasm in her words has pushed him to anger. But his tone is soft.

"You have strength. The prophecy speaks of it. I saw it with my eyes. But power does not mean you are ready for battle," he instructs.

There is something she sees in his eyes, but can't tell what it is. Like a memory or a flicker of a time filled with pain. He turns away and motions for her to follow. Tabatha stays close behind.

"Come, we can train up here."

"You know your way around here, don't you?" she asks, stepping over a bag where mice feast.

When Eli rounds the corner, they are in an open space. The sun streams in from the row of windows, illuminating barrels that are fresh with soot from recent fires.

"I have trained here many mornings and slept here most nights," he says, kicking bottles and trash from their path.

Sorrow pulls at her heart, watching Eli maneuver around the space with comfort. Seeing his tattered clothing and matted hair, she knew his journey was unpleasant, but walking where he used to lay his head makes her hurt for him.

"Follow my stance," he commands, jolting her from thought.

Eli shifts his feet and places his fists near his face. Trying to mimic his action, she places her feet apart and raises her arms. She assesses his stance, trying to better position herself when Eli lunges forward.

Screaming, she shifts her arms, crossing them in front of her face. Bracing for him to hurt her, she holds her breath, but the pain of the impact does not come. Feeling the slight push from his hands as Eli pats her shoulders, Tabatha opens her eyes.

"Well done, Tabatha. Your stance is firm. More training will strengthen your posture and prepare you to attack. Next time, keep your eyes open. You never know where death will strike."

Eli steps away, returning to his position. Tabatha mimics his actions, placing her feet further and adjusting her fists. Perspiration moistens the small of her back as she watches Eli. Anticipating his movements, she relaxes her posture. Eli lunges and Tabatha keeps her eyes open as he approaches. But this time she yelps as he pushes her, and Tabatha stumbles to the ground.

The concrete floor is cold and hard. The impact rattles through her. Landing on her fingers, they tingle and send a shooting pain up her arm. Rubbing her hand, Tabatha narrows her gaze as she watches him return to his training stance.

"Why did you push me?" she shouts, voice echoing off the barren walls. Mice scatter under her voice.

He ignores her question and provides instruction, "You kept your eyes open, but your feet should be like a tree. Firm and bending with the weight of my attack, but never falling."

"I didn't like that. Don't do it again."

"Up," he calls, waiting for her to rise.

Tabatha shakes her head, "No. That was mean, and you didn't do that the first time."

Eli relaxes his arms. He tilts his head, "I am unsure why you are surprised. As I said, you never know where death will strike. Expecting that I would react in the same manner was your error, not mine. Stand. Plant your feet and bend with my attack."

"No!" she says, pushing away from the ground. "I don't want to do this."

Upright and heading for the door, Tabatha stomps her feet. Eli's voice halts her.

"How long will you keep running?"

His words echo and send a chill through her. The words fill her ears and cause her skin to burn.

Angered, she shouts back, "You know nothing about me! You are just some strange man who thinks I'm special."

Tucked in her pocket, Tabatha's phone buzzes. Pulling it from her pants, she watches the screen glow, flashing Sam's name. Declining the call, she looks at Eli, who raises an eyebrow.

Stuffing the phone back in her pocket, she tells him, "That's not me running."

Eli closes the distance between them, "You may not be ready to accept that you are running, but you must accept this. When we are in this space, I am your mentor. I will not coddle you. I will ensure you are prepared to cross the portal and are ready to face what is on the other side."

Rolling her eyes, she turns from him.

"Where are you going?" he calls.

"To get breakfast. I'm sure you can't cross a portal on an empty stomach."

CHAPTER THIRTY-FIVE

35

Tabatha's eyes open and shut, trying to adjust to the light. Her nose widens, grateful for the fresh air filling her lungs. Free of the confines of the stifling factory walls, Tabatha stops to pull her hair from her tie. Releasing her curls feels like liberation. It feels like a release from Eli's expectations. It feels free.

Shaking herself, she rubs her bare arms that start to absorb the warmth of the sun and warming air. She turns her head toward the broken building and narrows her eyes. Turning away from the crumbling outer walls, she glances toward her feet. Muttering, she says, "I'm not running."

Feet planted firmly on the ground, she feels her toes twitch when Eli calls to her.

"Tabatha."

"No, Eli," she says, resisting the urge to sprint forward.

"Do not run, Tabatha."

"Why?" her voice is defiant, like a toddler.

"Tabatha, please. I am sorry."

His words surprise her, prompting her to turn to him. She observes him and the lack of anger he has when he approaches. She feels the absence of judgment and scolding, leaving her feeling puzzled.

"You're sorry?" she questions.

Tabatha steps toward him, and Eli closes the distance.

"It was wrong of me to thrust you into training with little explanation. I have come to learn of many differences between your world and mine. In this world, you are not born preparing for war. You know nothing of battle and how your enemy will do anything to get the upper hand. Tabatha, you are the Chosen One. You are powerful, but like I said, strength does not mean battle ready. I am sorry."

She observes the big man and his display of humility. His behaviors, the lack of anger, and the need for understanding make her smile.

"You know, right now, you look like my brother anytime he used to play too rough and was scared I would tell Mom," she chuckles.

Tabatha sees a smile emerge from under the tuff of his beard.

"I would imagine your mother was a formidable warrior," he says.

Her smile grows, filled with thoughts of her mother's strength, longing for it to flow through her, "She was."

"I pray the ancestors will allow me to meet her in the after realm."

Confused, she shakes her head and her curls tumble forward. Pushing fallen curls from her face, she asks, "What is the after realm?"

"It is the place after this world. Where are being goes to rest when our path in this world is over."

"That sounds pretty," Tabatha smiles. "My mother used to talk about ancestors when she was sick. When you said that, it reminded me of her."

The call of birds sings as the morning air turns warm. A butterfly floats between them, almost landing on Tabatha's nose. The playful creature makes her smile, and she shifts her attention to Eli.

"Slow. We take this slow. I don't want to end up on the ground or anything like that."

Eli nods and gestures toward the factory door, and Tabatha steps forward.

"I will save landing on the floor for one of our harder lessons," he grins.

Tabatha stops to glare at Eli.

Ignoring her warning scowl, Eli leads the way back into the stench of the factory.

The putrid odor makes her want to run away, so she asks Eli about the portal.

"You were talking about a portal. What is it? Do we have to go to some special place to find it?"

"I will open it when the time comes," Eli says, as they return to the open room. He takes his place a few paces from her in the empty factory room.

Tabatha places her hands on her hips and tilts her head to the side, "Eli, you want me to believe you are going to open a portal?"

"I will not fight with you to believe me, Tabatha. I will merely show you when it is time. Now follow my movements. I will teach your body how to become strong. Then you will learn to spar."

Ignoring his prompt, she presses on about the portal.

"How do we find where the best place is to open the portal? Do we have to find lay lines or search the library for ancient maps?"

Tabatha's eyes dance with wonder as she imagines them traipsing through halls and caves like an explorer.

Eli pinches the bridge of his nose, "In this world, you experience life in the wrong way. Relying on what you call science. Do you not feel the way fate pulls you? Listen to the flow of the land. Once you do that, you will understand where the energies are most strong."

"Well, how do I do that? Why can't we do that kind of training?" she huffs.

Eli ties his locs upon his head and urges Tabatha to do the same. Removing the hair tie from her wrist, she follows.

"You will learn that in my world, where the pull is much stronger. For now, please follow my instruction. We have at least an hour before we miss the best part of the morning."

"Oh yeah, what part is the best part?"

"The part before people awaken and mess it up."

CHAPTER THIRTY-SIX

36

After sneaking into the restaurant kitchen, Eli and Tabatha hide away in the apartment, eating their meal. Tabatha rocks back and forth on the couch, with Eli silently eating beside her.

Fatigue slows Tabatha's bites as she struggles to keep her eyes open. She blinks slower and heavier. When her eyes reopen, she feels the fork hanging from her mouth. Flicking her napkin at Eli, who smirks at her, she says, "Don't laugh at me. This is your fault."

He chuckles, "Do not feel ashamed. I remember training my tiny warriors. They could hardly open their mouths for the first meal after training. I remember the scolding their mother gave me. It still shakes me greater than any battle to think of it."

Tabatha watches as Eli's expression grows more distant as he reminisces.

"You have a family?" her words are like a whisper, unsure if they should be spoken or remain a thought.

When Eli meets her gaze, he lingers, as if trying to regain his bearings. Running his hands through his locs, he continues, "That was long ago. Your body will become accustomed to the fatigue as we continue training."

"Tell me about them." she presses, longing to see the flicker of light that glimmered in his expression.

"Move on, Tabatha."

She ignores the edge growing in his tone, "Please. I don't really know much about you, and you looked so happy for a moment. I—"

"I said, move on," he growls.

Tabatha pulls away, frightened by his scowl and the intensity in his body.

"I'm not your enemy," she stammers, trying to soothe the fury in his eyes that sends a chill through her veins.

Exhaling, he pushes himself from the couch and positions his back against the counter. His eyes intently focus on the door.

Tabatha shifts to see Eli, careful not to startle him. His face is void of expression; only his rising chest and tense fist reveal his struggle.

"Eli," she calls when the buzzing of her phone shakes her.

Sam's name flashes and she again declines. Turning the phone over, it buzzes. When she looks at the screen, she sees his message: Call me.

Powering her phone off, she looks at Eli. The rigidness of his body has eased, yet his face remains stoic. Like he has detached himself from his body and mind. It is as if he is just present.

Placing the phone down, she goes to his side. Eli does not recoil when she sits beside him. He does not push her away.

They focus on the door together, listening to the bustle of the street and the movement of the restaurant below. Eli flinches as the vent rattles, blowing cool air on them.

"I have a fiancé," she begins, not turning to see his expression. "That's the call I keep declining. It's a complicated situation. I don't love him. I don't even like him most days. But, he's good for me. He's good for my family. His connections could change so much, and I'd be doing my part by marrying him. I say that because I understand not wanting to talk about scary things."

Leaning her head against the counter, she catches Eli's expression, which has softened. He looks less distant, his body not as prepared to lash out. His eyes remain fixed on the door, but his hand moves. He gently pats her knee, then returns it to his lap.

The corners of her lips rise and fade as she remembers his words. The portal will open soon. Tugging at her sleeve, she wipes away a tear that slips from her eye. She is growing to enjoy his presence and isn't ready to lose him. To lose a genuine friend, something she hasn't had in a long time.

"I know about running, Tabatha. I am here because of it. But perhaps you can have the strength to defeat your demons, because I am proof you can't outrun them."

Tabatha does not push him for more, nor does she try to ease his pain. But she takes comfort in not feeling alone. A sensation that has not left her since her mother died.

"It's been years since Mom died. I've been so alone since then. I mean, I have my brother, but he's been distant. The only time I feel like he sees me is when I'm with Sam, my fiancé. I know I'm running. I don't want to run. I want to be strong. Strong like my mother taught me to be. Every day I held on to her bracelet, hoping it would remind me, push me, to be strong like her."

Tabatha's fingers reach for the bracelet that no longer dangles from her wrist. Eli shifts his gaze to her bare arm. Tabatha exhales, steadying her breath before she continues.

"Ever since that night, when I met you, I've been losing pieces of my loved ones. I walked away from Sam, which resulted in becoming further away from my brother and the last place I call home. I've never felt more lost."

Their eyes remain fixed on the door as the sun shifts, casting a rainbow of light through the glass panes.

"Maybe lost is a necessary destination to being found?" he says. The far-off expression returns to his face. Like he remembers a time and places far from where they sit. "I have lost my wife and four children on my journey to this world. But lost is how I found you and how I intend to find my way home. So perhaps we should not fear being lost, but merely embrace it."

Tabatha smiles, enjoying the thought of being found, "I think you're right, Eli. Maybe this adventure is about me finding myself and you finding your way back home."

When Tabatha turns to Eli, she spots a hint of a smile on his face, though it does not radiate joy or have any actual emotion behind it. Yet, it brings her comfort and assurance enough to rest her heavy eyes.

CHAPTER THIRTY-SEVEN

37

Time slips away, and sleep comes quickly for Tabatha next to Eli on the hard linoleum floor. Braced against the counter, releasing the fatigue of holding her world together makes her dreams peaceful and deep.

Tabatha, lost in a world of dreams, becomes disoriented when a sound rouses her. The sound is soft, and almost too hard to hear. It's infrequent, but when it comes, she can hear the cries of sharp agony.

It is Eli whimpering from his dreams.

Her eyes fly open, and Tabatha attempts to adjust to the darkened room. The glimmer of the moon offers enough light to shine on Eli's torn face. She watches as his body tightens and eases. She waits for the torment of his dreams to end, but his cries become louder and his grimace stronger. Beads of sweat drip from his brow.

"Eli," Tabatha calls, trying to rouse him.

Her words do not reach him as he becomes more tangled in the anguish of his nightmare. His body shakes and he groans.

Tabatha reaches to shake him, but his mumbling stops her.

"No, don't," he begs.

Not words spoken to her, but to whoever is in his dream. Yet, the words make her release her own cries of anguish. Tabatha feels sick with grief watching the man usually filled with bravado speaking with such a pained whimper. More sounds pour from his trembling lips, pleading for the pain to stop.

"Eli," Tabatha cries. But he does not wake.

She places a hand on his shoulder, hoping to draw him from his terror. But her actions send him into a panic. His eyes fly open. Frightened by the fury in his gaze, she draws away, but her sudden movement makes him strike quickly.

His fingers tighten around her shoulder, sending a wave of pain up her neck. Afraid to cry out, Tabatha silently stares as his mighty force knocks her down. She closes her eyes, preparing for the intense pain from his fist raised above her.

Tabatha, pinned to the floor, braces herself as she feels the rush of air as the blow comes down. But Eli does not strike her body. His fist strikes the floor beside her. She recoils, hearing the crack of his knuckles beside her ear. A grunt leaves his body as pain rises through his arm. Opening her eyes, she stiffens as she stares into Eli's horrified expression. A look that shows him in more anguish than when he was asleep.

Eli averts his eyes from her.

With his hand still locked on her shoulder, Eli's breathing slows as he becomes more present with reality. The pressure of his grip lightens, and he pulls away from her. When he speaks, his voice quivers. The sound frightens her to stillness.

"My apologies."

He speaks but does not bring himself to look at her. Staring up at him as the moon highlights his pain, she wishes for the black of night. Seeing his pain is almost too horrible to bear. Tabatha feels the tears welling in her eyes and tries to shift. Her movements send Eli from the floor.

His movements stop her as she becomes filled with paralyzing fear that her actions will cause him to strike. Tabatha remains motionless, even as Eli passes from her vision. She continues to be still until she hears his footfalls by the door.

Turning, Tabatha can see him exit out of the door and into the night. Exhaling, she realizes she was holding her breath. Then fear snatches her breath again when she considers, what if he never comes back?

CHAPTER THIRTY-EIGHT

38

The darkness of the night slowly disappears as the humid summer morning creeps in, bringing fresh worries as to why Eli has yet to return. Since Eli's departure, Tabatha has been pacing and checking her phone. As the sun rises higher and the temperature more stifling, Tabatha glances at her phone to check the time. She looks out the window, still no Eli.

Laying on the bed, she tries to sleep, but it does not come. With each passing voice in the alley, she strains to hear his commanding tone, only to be disappointed when the voices pass. She anxiously runs her fingers through her tousled curls as her stomach twists in knots.

"How did I go from wanting to get rid of you, to wanting you around?" she cries, wringing her hands together. She can not be still as the urge to do something grows. Shifting from the bed, she paces more then moves to the window.

Looking out the window, she sees Daniel enter the alley. Dropping to the floor, she listens for the heavy metal back door to close before she brings herself back to the window.

Days have gone by, and they haven't spoken a word, yet she still fears his anger.

"Where are you, Eli?" she says, searching the window.

"Fine, I'll have to go find you," she decides, unable to wait a moment longer for his return.

Gathering her things and heading down the back alley, she assesses her direction.

Eli has not mentioned how he spends his day when he is not with her, nor where he has been before their encounter.

"Think. What would Eli do?" tapping her forehead, she runs through their previous lessons. "He trains in the morning because few people are there. It's late afternoon. People will migrate back there."

Letting a breath into her palms warms the chill of her fingertips. The unease twisting in her stomach moves her to walk in an unset direction. Her mind fills with the images of Eli lost and alone.

"Lost!" the word is like electricity buzzing through her. "He found me when he was lost."

Tabatha sets off toward their fateful meeting. The park is blocks away, but she can not wait for a bus. She needs to find him to ensure he is safe. With each passing moment, vivid images of Eli wrapped in pain urge her forward.

"Please be okay," she breathes.

As the trees and streetlights come into view, Tabatha's feet skip forward, fueled by adrenaline and a need to see him. Rounding the corner, she searches deep within the park. She does not see Eli in the place where she was caught by the two boys or by the gates where they exited.

Afraid and on the verge of tears, she turns to leave, when she feels the rush of her heartbeat drumming in her ears. Seated on a bench away from the crowded street corner are his broad shoulders.

"Eli!" she shouts, closing the distance with quick steps. He does not respond to his name or the fear causing her voice to shake. Now, at his side, she slows her pace as she carefully assesses him. Sorrow overtakes her as she looks upon Eli, watching, but not seeing, what is ahead of him. Her knuckles strain as she grips the bench tighter. His locs and beard contain specks of nature. Tabatha swallows past the lump in her throat as she imagines Eli sleeping outside. When she takes a seat next to him, his gaze remains fixed on the road ahead.

Tabatha keeps her eyes on Eli moments longer, watching in despair as he does not acknowledge her presence or that of those passing in front of him. Keeping her distance on the other side of the bench, she speaks, soft and slow, "Eli, are you okay? I was worried about you."

Eli turns to her. His head moves, but it takes his eyes a moment to register her. To see who she is. His gaze does not fill with joy or the frantic amusement it did upon their first meeting. Eli looks at her like she is here, but unreachable.

He speaks, but his words hold no emotion, "I needed time away."

She reaches for him, and he pulls away as if her touch will wound him. Feeling her frown deepen, she tries to reach him with her words, "I want to hear everything. Tell me, I—"

"I have delayed your training," he interrupts. "It won't happen again. Our worlds will be in alignment soon. You need to be battle ready. Ready for home. Ready for Zodia. For battle."

He rattles off words, repeating his assignment, his eyes never filling with emotion.

"Eli, please talk to me," Tabatha reaches for him, but he moves from the bench.

"Come, we must rest, then we train. We train, then I open the portal, and then home."

He edges forward, with Tabatha not far behind, fearing he will become lost in the crowd of people headed in the opposite direction.

"Eli!" she calls as people bump into her and push her further away.

Moving past the bodies crashing into her, she catches up to him. Tabatha crosses his path, halting his steps.

"Talk to me," she demands.

Eli's eyes flicker, and for a moment, she sees him stare at her. Seeing her for the first moment since their reuniting. The flicker fades, and his stare becomes cold.

"There is nothing to talk about," he pushes forward.

"Why did you leave?" she questions. Her words go ignored by Eli and those rushing by.

His dismissal of her words wounds her more than not being seen by her brother or Sam.

Running behind him, desperate for him to acknowledge her, she shouts, "Eli, I was worried you left without me getting to say goodbye."

Twisting to her, he snarls, "Do not lecture me on being absent. Don't rebuke me because your tender feelings are hurt. Not when my family has suffered far worse. When my loved ones have been deprived of my presence for far longer than you. When neither of us could offer proper goodbyes."

Eli towers above Tabatha, his anger radiating from him feverishly, yet Tabatha does not cower. She sees beyond his menacing glare and distorted aggression to the pain glistening in his eyes.

"Is that why you were gone? Because you missed them?"

He recoils away from her, "Leave it alone, Tabatha."

Thunder sounds in the distance as people disappear into street cars and shops, preparing to escape the rain.

"Eli," she says, stopping him from turning away.

He looks at her as the rain drops. The droplets coating his face like tears wishing to fall. Tabatha shivers, unsure if it is from the chilling air or his stare.

Closing his eyes, he let out a breath. When his eyes open, he has tucked away his rage, replacing it with his mask-like expression.

"I am sorry, Tabatha. For both my behavior last night and my anger at this moment. My mind has much to ponder, some of which never leaves me. Come, this chill will not be good for either of us."

This time, when Eli turns away from her, he looks back to ensure she follows. He offers a smile that peaks through the gruff of his beard but does not reach further. Tabatha steps forward, walking by his side, but not from the notion that he is the first one she will save.

CHAPTER THIRTY-NINE

39

Waking before her mentor, Tabatha places a warm cinnamon bun on a plate and wafts it by Eli's nose. She watches as his face twitches, roused by the cinnamony aroma. His eyes widen, and his lips salivate.

"What is that?" he murmurs, his eyes dilating with lust.

"Mikey's hot cinnamon buns, fresh off the cart. Wash up while they're hot."

Moving to the counter, she sets down the gooey, cinnamon-filled delights.

Eli walks over, assessing her. His eyes narrow as he closes into her.

"Personal space, please. Especially when you still smell like outside."

Eli backs away, but his gaze remains skeptical as he questions her, "What is wrong? I am the one to rouse you for our training, but you are alert, dressed, and offer breakfast."

Tabatha bats her eyes playfully, but he does not waiver. Rolling her eyes, she confesses. "Okay. I have an idea. But you can't say no."

"No," he says, moving toward the bathroom.

"Eli!" she says, following him. "You haven't even heard what I am proposing."

"We've already made too many deviations from your training. We can not afford another."

"I have listened to you regardless of whether I have agreed with what you said. Please do the same for me."

Arms braced on the bathroom doorframe; he sighs but looks at her. Tabatha smiles when she sees his brow raise, encouraging her to continue.

Clasping her hands together, she exclaims, "I'm going to train you today!"

He laughs, "I am not the one unfit for battle."

"No, but you are unfit for life. If you're not brooding, you are scolding me, or worried about something."

"There are many things to worry about, Tabatha."

"Yes, but there are also many things to smile about. All I'm asking for is one day to show you that. If you aren't satisfied by the end of today, I'll do double training, no triple. Deal?"

Tabatha crosses her fingers as Eli weighs her words.

When he shrugs, she is not sure if amusement or exhaustion has swayed him, but she twirls in victory. Not one to let her joy go unchecked, Eli speaks, "Do not rejoice yet. I will go along for a day. If you fail, do not think I won't make good on your bargain to do extra training."

Her smirk widens, "Yay, okay, hurry and get dressed. And don't think I won't eat your Mikey's if you take too long."

Eli groans and offers muffled complaints as he closes the bathroom door, leaving Tabatha giddy and ready to teach him his own lesson.

"This is foolishness," Eli snips as they walk down the city streets lined with row houses. Buildings to their right and left are filled with those returning from their night shift or windows empty of glass panes.

"It's training," Tabatha says, wiping sweat from her forehead. The sun barely shines over the horizon, but the asphalt is already hot.

Beside her, Eli grumbles and mutters, but his demeanor makes her laugh, "Is this really so hard for you? Eli, when was the last time you did anything other than train?"

"Training is a daily necessity, Tabatha."

She rolls her eyes, "If you get one thing out of today, I hope you realize how much of a pain you are when we train."

"I will take pleasure in having you run extra laps."

"Uh-uh, only if my training isn't effective. That's the deal," she says, wagging her finger.

"Tell me, what is our first task?"

"Give it some time," she says, checking her watch. Tabatha takes a seat on a bench that stands in between a chained-off basketball court and apartments almost unfit to live in.

Tabatha's face lights up when the door three houses down creaks open, revealing a salt and pepper afro'd man. Eli looks on as Tabatha turns her head toward the man.

"Take your shoes off, but hold on to them. Shoes walk in this part of town."

Tabatha slips out of her sneakers but keeps her feet from the hot asphalt as she watches the man approaching the hydrant. She waves, and he waves back. Pulling a wrench from his back pocket, he goes to work on the hydrant.

"That's Mr. Kroger. When I was a kid, everyone knew him as the Water Man. He never forgot to open the hydrants on hot summer days. It used to be the city's responsibility, but when the neighborhood deteriorated, those in power abandoned their commitment and left the community to fend for itself. Thankfully, people like Mr. Kroger step up to fill the gaps with acts of small kindness that bring joy and relief in these tough times."

"I do not understand. Why am I taking my shoes off?"

Tabatha looks at him, puzzled, "You have never played in the fire hydrant water? It's like dancing in the rain, but better."

Eli watches Mr. Kroger as the water gushes into the street, "We do not have fire hydrants."

Choosing to ignore his response, Tabatha hops from one foot to the next. She points to Eli's shoes, "Hurry up and take them off."

Groaning, he takes off his shoes.

"Good job, see, not so bad. Now come on."

Reaching the fire hydrant, Tabatha grabs Eli and pulls him into the water. As Tabatha dances in the water, her laughter is loud and effervescent. She spins around, watching as the sun creates rainbows in the droplets. When she turns to Eli, she pouts playfully. The big man stands, arms folded, as water pools at his feet.

"Don't be a big grumpy. This is about fun."

"I would have more fun if we were training."

A child comes from his front stoop and splashes in the puddle. The enormous leap creates a splash that lands on Eli's feet.

Jumping further away, Eli trips and lands in the path of the streaming water, drenching his pants. He huffs, while Tabatha and the child, missing two front teeth, laugh. The boy, who looks miniature next to Eli, wears a shirt that says, Robot King.

The laughing subsides, and Eli stomps his foot, splashing Tabatha and Robot King. Tabatha winks at the boy, and they leap into a puddle. Eli dodges their blast, but the battle of puddle splashes begins.

Their laughter fills the streets, bringing more people from their homes. Children line the sidewalk waiting for a turn, and aunties wearing sundresses take shade under the overhang. Eli's beard drips, and Tabatha's hair tightly coils by the time they exit.

"That wasn't so bad, was it?" she says, shaking her head to the tune of children playing and flip-flops slapping the ground.

"It was nice. But it is not training. Let us dry off and begin—"

"Oh, no," she interrupts. "I still have time to show you my kind of training. With this heat, we'll dry off soon enough."

"Where are you taking me now, Tabatha?" he groans.

"It's a surprise," she teases, showing him the way to their next destination.

CHAPTER FORTY

40

The blistering sun casts welcome shadows over the towering buildings and complexes, offering respite from its sweltering rays. Leaving the comfort of the shade, Tabatha points to an ice cream truck, "Have you been here?"

Wiping away the perspiration dripping from his brow, Eli motions no.

"This is the best ice cream. The owner's name is Pops. He has the expected icees and bars but also makes his own ice cream. We are going to get two cones."

"How is this training?"

She shrugs, "It's just fun."

Eli rubs his face.

"I still have hope that I will get rid of Mr. Grumpy and show you how to have a good time."

"There will be time for fun when there is peace."

"Well, I think we should always make room for fun while we wait for peace."

They reach the front of the line, and Pop's eyes widen.

"Oh, big fella there. What can I do for ya?" calls Pops, leaning in the window.

"Two cones with chocolate dip, please," Tabatha says.

"You bet it, pretty lady."

He disappears inside the truck, and Tabatha nudges Eli, "Would it kill you to smile? Try it when Pops hands you the ice cream. And make sure you say thank you. Even grumpies should have manners."

Rolling his eyes, Eli obliges her request when Pops returns. He forces a smile that looks almost painful. Eli says, "Thank You."

Pops shivers when he passes them their cones.

Tabatha laughs, leading Eli away from the truck, "Good job, but I think Pops is glad he doesn't have to look at that face anymore. Now one last spot, and then you can tell me how I did."

Eli bites through the crunchy chocolate coating and moans.

"I told you it's good!"

Eli takes another bite. "It is not bad," he says cooly, keeping a half smile on his face.

They finish the last of their cones and arrive at the top of a hill.

Taking a seat, Tabatha pats the ground for Eli to join her. A little less begrudgingly than before, he takes his place beside her. Looking out from the hilltop, they see the vast landscape of buildings, smog, and desperation.

The wind blows softly, cooling their warm skin. Amidst birds fluttering is the sound of the city's mixtape of buses, yelling, and horns blaring.

Feeling the way the sun prickles her skin, Tabatha recalls a memory, "I used to be afraid of the sun."

"Did you also have a Crimson Sun?"

She shakes her head, "No. I lived here for a while after Mom died. It still had half-broken apartments and crowded spaces, but I went to school in the upper east, where all the rich kids live. Oddly enough, I can be quite smart sometimes. The problem, though, was few people looked like me there. My skin always fascinated them. In the summer, they always came up to me and compared how dark my skin was to theirs. They used to comment about it so much I would wear long sleeves and stand in the shade at recess to hide. So I guess we both have a sun we are battling."

Eli listens intently as Tabatha drifts to a memory as he has done frequently. Pulling herself from the thoughts, she looks into his assessing eyes, "Tell me something about you, Eli. Something that isn't sad or about war."

He takes a moment to reflect, sifting through thoughts he had long forgotten. His mind strays down paths of the past, stirring emotions he assumed were lost. Yet, the memories remain vivid and clear, reminding him of days gone by.

The memory becomes fuller, leaving a smirk on his lips and life in his eyes, "Alora, my oldest, she's a spitfire like her mother. She wanted to make breakfast for her siblings, mother, and me. The youngest, Jane, was recently born, and the house was tired from endless nights of her crying. But not Alora; she woke early, cracking eggs and mixing batter to make a large breakfast as her mother does. Except, she was too young to maneuver the stove and fire properly. The flame engulfed the kitchen, nearly burning down the house. It took months to get the smell of char out of the walls. But I still remember her sooty face streaked with tears. She was terrified we would scold her, but all her mother and I could do was wrap her in our arms. We were grateful we didn't lose her or any of our children. The funniest thing about the situation was my wife had been pestering me about kitchen repairs. We joke she and Alora conspired to burn down the kitchen, to hurry the improvements."

Eli laughs. The sound is light but real. It is the first time Tabatha sees the life in his eyes linger. She watches as the glimmer of peace washes over his usually war-torn face.

Smiling, she asks, "Are you ready for your last training exercise?"

He groans, albeit more playfully this time, "What is it?"

Her smile broadens, turning more devious and spirited, "We are going to roll down this hill."

"Why would we do that?"

"Because it's quicker than walking down."

This time Eli does not resist. Shrugging, he gets into position.

"I'll race you down," he says, rolling first down the hill.

"Cheater!" Tabatha calls, rolling after.

They tumble, laughing and yelling all the way down. When they reach the bottom, and the world spins less frantically, they remain laughing and wiping tears from their eyes.

"I think that's an actual laugh that time. No more, Mr. Grumpy."

This gets another roar of laughter from Eli, who grasps his belly.

"Fine, fair enough," he says in between bursts of laughter. "What was the purpose of this, Tabatha?"

His laughter fills the space, while she turns more serious, "You look so pained all the time. Like happiness is something to be afraid of. I wanted to remind you what it felt like."

Eli's smile and the light that touches his eyes remain, "It would seem the teacher can learn from the student."

Tabatha dances, celebrating her victory.

With a smile on his face, he says, "Allow me to offer you one lesson, if that is okay?"

"Come on," she groans. But her pouting does not waiver his countenance.

He continues, "You should care for yourself as much as you do for others. Do not allow anyone to push you into a corner you do not wish to be in."

Her eyes glisten at the sincerity of his words.

"Thank you," she whispers. Holding back tears, she wraps Eli into an embrace. He relaxes into her and wraps an arm around her before ruffling her curls.

"Eli!" she groans, pushing him back.

"I am not the only one with leaves and twigs in my hair."

"Oh, is that a joke I hear?" she teases.

Sticking his hands in his pockets, he nudges her gently as they begin their walk home.

"Hey, Eli. You think since you are no longer a grumpy, it's time to look less...." her words trail off as she gestures to his tangled locs and matted beard.

He stops, touching his head and face, "I had forgotten about this. At first, it was a matter of convenience, then a tool that kept others away."

"Do you think you still need those?" she asks, careful not to offend him.

He smiles, and her concern eases.

"Will you help me, Tabatha?"

Nodding, she says, "Race you home."

Taking off, she hears Eli complaining behind her. Relieved he is at her back, she allows her tears to fall.

Tabatha longs to tell Eli how she appreciates having a brother again but worries her words will only make his departure that much more painful.

CHAPTER FORTY-ONE

41

It's a new day, and yesterday's laughter is now filled with orders from Eli. Training has gone on for hours this morning, with Tabatha landing on the floor for most of it.

"Get out your head and into your body. Your opponent can't see your thoughts, but they will see your fear."

Tabatha glowers at Eli, who has knocked her down once again. Today, he wields a stick he found during their walk to training. The stick, long and broad, has become her archenemy this morning, as Eli uses it to repeatedly knock her to the ground. This time, he did so because she was moving too slowly.

Eli, freshly shaven and trimmed, circles Tabatha. As Tabatha thinks back to the night before, she regrets not nicking him a time or two during their impromptu barber session for the annoyance he now causes her. While Eli circles her with a smile, it annoys her more than his typical scowl.

He rests his training stick across his shoulders as he taunts her, "If you are mad I knocked you down, rise and strike."

Growling, Tabatha pounds the ground, "I can't!"

"You can. Up!"

His words echo off the empty factory walls, scurrying mice into hiding. His forceful demeanor once sent shivers through Tabatha, but now fill her with annoyance and makes her teeth grind.

Pushing herself from the ground, her unsteady feet brace for another attack. She has perfected the stance Eli has shown her, but the tremor of her fists betrays her fatigue.

Eli lunges forward, this time swatting her shoulder harder than he did the last time. Tabatha cries out; a tear falls from her eyes. Reaching for her shoulder, she shudders at the sensation of helplessness.

Tabatha is not afraid of Eli, but she knows she can not defeat him.

Seeing the wavering in her eyes, he speaks, "Come at me, Tabatha."

Her head shakes violently as her throbbing shoulder pulses.

"Come at me fiercely," he growls, pounding the stick on the ground. His words are meant to spur her to action, yet they only ground her more.

The echo of his voice sends shivers through her. Tabatha's eyes shift to the exit, but Eli steps in her path. Her limbs tremble as they did that night in the park, caught between the boys who taunted her. The night Eli came into her life.

"I'm tired and hurt. I can't do this," she whimpers as her tears moisten the concrete floor. Her shaking pushes past her fingers and seeps into her bones, causes all of her to rattle.

"Your feelings do not matter on the battlefield. You must know you can do this. Strike at me, Tabatha."

Her body shivers with fear as she does not see her mentor. Tabatha only sees a menacing opponent willing to harm her. She looks into his eyes for guidance, but she sees the stony stare of a warrior engrossed in battle.

Eli approaches her, and she cowers into a ball. Her body trembles, waiting for the next painful strike.

She knows his intent is to teach her to be strong, but fear reminds her of how weak she is. Fear tells her to run.

"Look at me," he says, his voice now a soft whisper. Her eyes shift to him, but she does not leave her protective posture.

"Show me what lies beyond the fear. I see it, the anger you try to hide. The power begging to be released. Show it to me, Tabatha. Better yet, show it to yourself."

Her shaking body rattles her teeth, stuttering her speech, "I-I am j-just some girl who—"

He stops her, "You are not some girl. Show me who you are."

The calmness of his tone relaxes her body from its huddle.

She wants to be strong. To fight against the fear holding her in place, but her failures remind her to be careful of trying.

Casting the stick to the side, Eli lunges forward, "Show me how strong you are, Tabatha, or prepare to die."

Eli raises his hand, ready to land a final blow. Tabatha watches the balled fist come toward her head.

Determination beats like the pulse of her heart as instinct pushes her to survive.

"No!" she screams. Shooting her hands above her head, she blocks his blow.

She blinks, stunned at how her body sprung to action.

"Good. Push me back," Eli instructs.

Tabatha pushes, sending his hand back.

"Forward," he instructs.

Full of determination, she follows his command, stepping toward him. Eli moves back, but she follows. With each step, confidence grows.

"Good. Strike. Do not think. Strike!"

Tabatha acts, lunging one fist, then the next. Eli catches each thrust in the palm of his hand. Her attacks increase as her movements become more fluid.

Tabatha swings harder with each block. She plants her feet as he has taught her and shifts her hip to control the power and direction. Her body moves with strength, pushing him back with each attack.

Her movements increase in speed and intensity until Eli's back is against the wall. With nowhere left to move, she thrusts and yells, releasing a barrage of uncontrollable punches.

She fights against Eli and days of agonizing training. She attacks harder, knocking away each thought of her brother's words or Sam's actions that fill her mind. Tabatha hits again, releasing the grief and anger she has masked after losing her mother.

She strikes again, her tears flowing as fear of losing someone important to her fuels her rage. One blow connects with Eli's collarbone. The sharp throbbing of the bone-on-bone impact slows her movements, but not her tears. Her tears release, and her body quivers as adrenaline leaves her body exhausted.

Her hands press against her eyes as if to push the pain inside, yet it refuses to yield to her attempt to hide any longer. The tears slip through her fingers and run down her arm.

Eli steps forward and wraps her in an embrace. Tabatha tries to pull away, but he holds her tighter, "Well done. I knew there was a fire within you."

Tabatha shudders, wrapping her arms around him. Holding on tight, she listens to the steady beat of his heart, its rhythm slowing her tears.

Steadiness returns to her legs, and she pulls away from him. Using the sleeve of her shirt, Tabatha wipes the last of her tears. She looks at Eli, who smiles proudly.

She narrows her red puffy eyes and groans playfully, "My mentor sucks, you know that?"

His chuckle is low and is a welcome echo in the quiet room, "You strike like lightning. I will have a bruise in the coming days."

"You deserve it after what you've put me through."

He grins, "Perhaps. But, now that you have your fire, let's see if you can keep it. Hand me my stick. We go again."

CHAPTER FORTY-TWO

42

Following training, Tabatha departs from Eli to sort through her feelings. Her victories during today's sparing match leave her body weary and her heart heavy. Stepping past her mother's restaurant, her feet know where she must go, even before her mind has made the choice.

It's a crowded street as people hurriedly push their way to lunch. Despite the crowd noisily talking on their phones and the scream of bus breaks, Tabatha's world is silent.

The once watchful woman, careful to move from coming traffic, walks as if no one is around. Her steps against the concrete reverberate through her as her world moves slowly, like a shell watching as someone else takes control.

When Tabatha reaches her destination and her fingers touch the rusted gate, her heart skips faster. Her mind realizes where her feet have brought her. The gate cries out as it scrapes against the ground. She is not sure if it is an eerie welcome or a warning to turn back.

Its rotted appearance of the gate matches the brokenness of the abandoned church. A place once filled with hope, now is abandoned and empty.

It has been years since Tabatha stepped foot on these grounds, yet she never forgot the place where her mother lay. For years, the thought of returning to the gravesite filled her with terror. Despite the tremble in her fingers and the beat of her heart, this place fills her with agonizing numbness.

The cemetery rests in the shadows of moss-covered trees and towering buildings. The grounds are nestled in the bustling city, yet there is an eerie presence of loneliness that is amplified by the overgrown grass and lack of flowers on graves.

Tabatha makes her way through the graveyard, her eyes lingering on each gravestone until they settle on her mother's. Moss covers the headstone, but Tabatha can clearly see her name, Hope Eshete.

The numbness fades as she succumbs to the reality of her mother's passing. The well of grief she hides behind the mask of optimism has faded. What remains is misplaced anger, threaded by lingering questions, that makes her drop to her knees.

"Why? Why couldn't you get better? You could fix anything. Why couldn't you fix yourself?"

In her mind, she rationalizes her mother's illness, knowing she could have done little to stop its effects, yet the hurt she keeps hidden within demands answers.

She snuggles closer to the mossy stone, longing for her mother's embrace, but only receives the cold earth beneath her fingers.

"When you were dying, you told me you wouldn't be here. You said you'll be walking among the ancestors, but I wish that wasn't true. I want you right here with me."

Her words stop as her throat tightens and tears drip onto her lips. She doesn't fight against them as they pour. She doesn't run from the fear and pain. Tabatha allows her sobs to turn into wailing for all the years of missing her mother and for losing all the reminders of her.

Tabatha's fingers stroke her wrist. As the tears subside, she feels less lonely without the charms and comforted by the memories that remain. Leaning her body against the solid stone, she quietly rocks back and forth. Tabatha relaxes into the soothing warmth traveling up her spine from the grave marker, heated by the gentle rays of the sun.

Tilting her head back, she looks to the sky, "There's so much I want to tell you. I don't even know where to begin. But I'll try."

Tabatha's words flow as easily as her questions. She tells her mother about the state of the diner, and her relationships with her brother and Sam. When she tells her mother about Eli, she smiles.

"You wouldn't believe half the things he says. He talks about this other world called Zodia and about portals. Can you believe it? I think he's having some mental breakdown or something, but he's fun to be around. But I'm afraid. I think this portal means he's going back to his family or leaving. He calls me the Chosen One. I think that means he enjoys having me around. I know I wanted him out of my life, but he reminds me of how things used to be between Daniel and me."

Thunder rumbles in the distance.

Tabatha's smile fades at the sound of the far-away rumbles, knowing she will soon have to go. She lies against the warm stone, enjoying the warmth as if it were her mother's embrace. The wind blows, carrying the fresh scent of approaching rain. The trees rustle, and Tabatha smiles.

"If I close my eyes, it sounds like your bangles making music with each step."

The rustling stops, and the sun fades behind the clouds. Tabatha stands. Placing a hand to her lips and then on the top of the gravestone, she says goodbye, "I love you, Mom. Sorry, it took so long, but I'll be back soon."

She steps away and reaches the creaking wail from the gate that fills her with less fear than when she entered. As Tabatha steps further away, she longs for the creaking reminder signaling her return.

Heading back toward the restaurant, the wind whips, and the rumble of thunder grows louder. The diner comes into view, and Tabatha looks away as the wind whirls. She shields her face from the chilling blast, and a shiver runs through her. When Tabatha turns her head back to the road ahead, another icy wave runs through her veins. But this time, it is not the elements that make her grow cold and drain the feeling from her body.

Her eyes grow wide as she darts her head, looking for somewhere to hide, because Sam is standing right in front of her.

CHAPTER FORTY-THREE

43

Tabatha looks up and down the empty street, desperate for someone to come to her aid. But the grey clouds have ushered people from the pavements. She darts her eyes, looking for a place to escape. She takes a step to move around him, but Sam is like a wall, closing in with each of her steps.

"Where have you been?"

His words send tremors through her. The cold callousness of his words sends her back to being under his thumb.

"You leave in the middle of the night, then don't answer my calls."

Tabatha ignores his words as she listens for the heavy footfalls of Eli, but she can hear nothing but the drumming of her heart beating in her ears. Running in the night was easy, but walking away in the brightness of day with Sam glaring at her, wanting her to stay, is a battle she is not sure she is ready to face.

"I just visited your brother looking for you. Imagine how surprised he was when I told him I hadn't seen you. Where have you been, Tabatha?"

Her breath comes quickly as panic courses through her. She feels as trapped as she did sitting inches away from him, searching for a ring she has no desire to wear.

"Tabatha!"

"I don't know," she shouts, trying to inch away from him.

The clouds overhead darken, and thunder rumbles closer.

"Unbelievable. Is anything ever simple with you? Let's go," he says, stepping toward her.

Tabatha steps away.

Sam's lips twist, revealing his anger, "I'm not staying here to get caught in the storm. Let's go."

"No," she says. The defiance in her voice stirs her. She can feel the strength in her soul as Sam looks at her. His eyes raise, surprised she does not comply.

"I'm willing to ignore these past few days, but not if you're going to be difficult," he breathes, trying to regain control.

Feeling the fire of her mother and the desire to show her strength, she plants her feet, "I'm not going with you. Not now, not ever. I know that comes as a surprise because I never said I didn't want this, not really, but I don't, Sam. I don't want to marry you."

Sam looks at her, really looks at her, like he sees all of who Tabatha is; her strength, her vulnerability, and her meekness. Tabatha stares back, and when he is about to speak, she continues, "I've made you to be the villain, but that's not true. The villain was me. I wasn't honest with myself. I just followed, and now it's time for me to lead."

Sam shifts, and for a moment, Tabatha thinks he understands her words. She prepares to be accepted by him, but his annoyance shifts to rage. "I'm getting what's mine," he growls, reaching for her.

His movements are swift, and his grip tightens as he wraps his fingers around Tabatha's wrists. Her breath quickens in response. Sam tries to pull her toward him, but she stands her ground, refusing to be moved. A flicker of frustration crosses Sam's face as his hand reaches for her shoulder, desperate to maintain control. As his hand tightens its grip on her shoulder, Tabatha's training kicks in, urging her to take action.

Though his hold is firm, Tabatha remains steadfast. With a quick shift of her feet and a forceful grasp at the base of his wrist, she manages to halt his attempt to draw her closer. The strain on Sam's face intensifies as he struggles against her resistance.

Undeterred, he pulls again, but this time she steps forward with the force of his motion. The sudden release of tension catches him off guard, causing him to stumble backwards. Seizing the opportunity, Tabatha swiftly twists free from his weakened grip. Taking her opportunity, she sidesteps out of his reach.

"I am not yours," she says as her nose flares. Her lungs beg for air following the rush of movement as intensity of their encounter.

Sam turns to her, his look more puzzled than before, "I'm not talking about you being mine."

Thunder rumbles louder, and a raindrop falls, landing on her cheek.

"Why would I want you? You're clumsy, a dreamer, ruin everything and need others to clean up your mess. You don't even see what's in front of you."

Tabatha watches as Sam taunts her ignorance. She watches his grin widen, and eyes dance. He takes pleasure in knowing that his words hurt her and that she is unaware of what she has lost. Tabatha searches for an answer, but he continues, revealing a worse fate than anything she could imagine, "This whole time, you thought I put up with you because it gets me closer to the restaurant, but it's already mine."

Tabatha feels a burning in her chest. Unable to comprehend his words, she says, "What do you mean?"

He laughs, relishing in her confusion. Tabatha, at the mercy of his words, waits for him to continue, "Daniel had complete control over Hope's Diner... until he couldn't pay the rent. When that happened, I took the opportunity to propose a deal: I would acquire the diner, and he could be in charge of the daily operations, and in exchange, I consider taking you as a wife. Sounds like a sweet deal, doesn't it? A great investment for me— plus, I can get rid of my maid. But with your recent behavior, I'm starting to think that perhaps I should just keep hold of the restaurant after all."

Feeling sick and dizzy, she places her hands on her knees to steady herself. Tabatha's breathing comes short and shallow as she tries to regain her breath. She sees Sam's feet come into view. She hears the gloating in his voice as he bends next to her, "It would have been a cute story, me marrying the daughter of a failing restaurant. Restoring it with you by my side. But now, I'll make sure I get rid of every remnant of your mother, starting with your brother."

Lightning flashes, and rain pours. Sam pulls away from her, and she hears a vehicle pulling up beside them. Tabatha stands, watching Sam get into the taxi. She feels a numbness creep up from her toes. A coldness that she feels in the depth of her soul. A fear that makes her feel smaller than she has ever been.

Sam sees this. Tabatha can tell from the glimmer in his eyes and the curl of his lips. He calls to her, and the joy in his tone makes her ill.

"If you're home by the end of the week, I might change my mind. You're a decent cook. But if you decide to have another bright idea, like leaving again, I'll make sure my lawyers drain you and your brother of everything you have left. No matter how small that is."

The door shuts, and the taxi pulls away, leaving her alone in the increasing downpour. The heaviness of her wet clothing fails to compare to the weight of Sam's words and her brother's betrayal.

Tabatha feels the pain of darkness being lifted as gentle fingers guide her away from despair. A sheltering umbrella unfurls above, providing solace and protection from the rain. Tabatha looks up to find Eli.

"Eli," she whispers.

The big man is by her side. His eyes dance with delight as he guides her from the rain, "I saw the clouds and was worried you'd get caught in the rain. When I went to look for you, I saw you and that man. You evaded him like an experienced warrior. You should be proud. Now, let's get you out of the rain."

CHAPTER FORTY-FOUR

44

The walk to the apartment is like moving through a dream. A mix of blurred images and words too hard to grasp. Tabatha's body shakes from the chill of a summer storm and the weariness of a broken heart.

She feels her heavy wet body drift to her bed, but Eli guides her away, "It's okay."

She hears his words, but they seem far from her.

Nothing seems okay as her mind replays Sam's ultimatum. Would there be any okay with Sam's threat and her brother's betrayal? She wonders if anything exists that could help her feel less trapped than she does at this moment.

Eli says more words that Tabatha has trouble making out. The words shower and rest float into her ears, but she can't place them in the right order.

When she feels the warmth of the shower beating on her face, it helps to draw her from the haze. Her limbs feel less like lead as she moves from the bathroom and nestles herself into comforting sheets.

Tabatha's eyes blink heavily as she watches Eli remove the electric kettle from the cupboard. Her eyes drift closed for longer and longer.

Each time they reopen, Eli is in a different position until he appears at her bedside with a steaming cup.

His hand reaches around her, helping to lift her. When Tabatha is seated, Eli offers her the drink, "Here, focus on the warmth of the cup and the burn as you sip. It will help your mind and soul recover from the intensity it felt when you were in battle."

Sipping the liquid, the heat burns her lips and then her throat. The tea is sweet, like honey, and leaves a smoky taste on her lips. Wincing, she blinks as her fingers tap the warm cup. After a few more sips, Tabatha is able to speak.

"I wouldn't call that battle," she squeaks as the steam warms her nose.

Eli moves to the edge of the couch, drinking his own cup of tea.

"You were up against a rival, and you had to use your wits and tactics to put some space between you. That is the nature of battle, Tabatha. The weariness that you are feeling comes from engaging in combat. Shifting your mind from that moment will help both your body and soul recover."

Tabatha continues to nurse her drink, allowing it to soothe her, as he instructed.

The amber-colored liquid leaves a bitter taste on her tongue and warmth that eases her mind.

"What is this?" she asks.

Eli sets his cup on the table, "I found tea and whisky in the kitchen. In this world, your ale is not as strong, but I've learned with enough, it can make the longest days easier."

She smiles, enjoying the thought of Eli doing something as normal as savoring a drink with friends.

Tabatha takes another sip and stares into the bottom of her mug. She turns toward the creak of the couch as Eli moves to take her cup.

"Rest," he says. "Tomorrow will be here soon, and we will return to training."

She smiles, "Thank you, Eli."

Eli moves to the kitchen, dropping the cups into the sink. Tabatha draws the blanket closer. When she closes her eyes, the images replay. Forcing her eyes open, she asks Eli another question, "Why didn't you step in? If you saw me, why'd you watch?"

Eli unfolds the blanket lying on the end of the couch and pulls it over him as he settles on the chair, "You seemed like you had it under control."

"It didn't feel like I was in control."

She hears him hum and watches his eyes close. His toes hang from the couch, which is too small for his large body.

Tabatha tries to follow her mentor and shuts her eyes, but images of Daniel and Sam conspiring about the restaurant cause her to wake.

"Eli."

"Tabatha?" he grumbles.

Her eyes fill with tears as pain grips her heart. She swipes them away and clears her throat, "Do you think family can move on from anything?"

Her words slip out, filled with fear. Tabatha is unsure if she can ever forgive her brother's actions. She nibbles on her lip, anxious about what Eli will say.

The rain beats against the window pane, and the wind whistles. The couch groans as Eli sits forward.

"I have pondered that question many nights. I have no answer, only hope that when I return home, the answer is favorable."

Tabatha smiles at him, "I hope you find out soon."

Eli grins, "I will. It will not be long before it is time to reopen the portal."

Eli lays back, and the patter of rain fills the silence.

"Was that person family?" he asks.

Tabatha pauses, unsure what Sam is. Rival felt more appropriate, but if she wished to keep her mother's restaurant safe, Sam would have to be more.

The howling of the wind eases, and the rain transitions to a gentle pattern.

"He is the one I have been avoiding. The calls I ignore. But I don't think I can ignore him much longer."

Eli's sigh is loud and deep. He rises again, and they meet each other's eyes. She sees the depth of concern and mutual understanding as he speaks, "Tabatha, we have days that remain. I urge you to settle whatever is lingering. I have had enough restless nights about things of the past to know it is best to settle things before leaving."

Eli nods, and Tabatha returns the gesture. He settles on the couch, and Tabatha calls to him once more, "Eli, I'm glad you're on the couch and not the floor. Goodnight."

His low chuckle makes her smile, and the room grows quiet as he sinks into sleep. Tabatha remains awake as the rain stops and silence fills the room. The room grows darker as she explores how she will keep her freedom and save everyone who needs her.

Eli insists she must cross the portal to save his world, but she realizes this is only his fantasy. He will depart, and she will have to choose between securing her own future and preserving her mother's legacy.

Tabatha's eyelids flutter as she descends into a heavy sleep, her thoughts full of unresolved anxieties. Before she fades into the darkness of dreams, she can't help but feel a sense of dread, knowing that by the end of the week, someone close to her will be disappointed.

CHAPTER FORTY-FIVE

45

Tabatha edges closer to the ultimatum from Sam each day. Deep in thought, she spends long hours contemplating her next move, weighed down by the implications of her choice. Her sleepless nights blur into days, passing before her in a haze.

When Eli speaks, Tabatha finds it difficult to pay attention. He speaks daily of the portal and returning to his people, but Tabatha misses much of the conversation. Eli says it will be soon, but the only timeline she can grasp is Sam's deadline.

Eli's sharp battle cry removes her from her haze. The sound echoes in the space, which has become her second home. Sunlight streams through the factory windows as mice scurry from their distracting sounds.

Springing into action, Tabatha's attention shifts to Eli as he sprints toward her. He closes the distance and brings his hand down, connecting with Tabatha's braced arms raised above her head. She is prepared and strong, unmoved by his attack.

He grins. Shifting his hands, he grabs her shoulders, and she does the same to him.

Remembering his instruction, she grasps him in this way to avoid being brought to the ground. She plants her feet and sways like a tree in a windstorm, as Eli pulls her to the left, then to the right.

"Well done, Tabatha," he praises before sweeping his foot to hers. He releases her shoulders, and she falls to the ground.

Scowling, she says, "We didn't practice that!"

"Practice is not the reason I brought you down. Your mind and body are not aligned. Speak. What is on your mind?"

She looks away. Tabatha doesn't want to discuss the troubles in her mind. She only wishes to push them away. To hide until they no longer exist.

Rubbing her bottom, which did little to protect her from the fall, she probes Eli about the portal.

"Remind me again. Can the portal open anywhere?"

"Yes. It is not about location, but about the alignment of elements. During the new moon in Leo, this world and mine will be in the best position to open a portal."

"Why? What's special about the Leo season?"

"This is the time of new beginnings."

Tabatha huffs, "Doesn't this sound strange to you?"

When Eli turns to her, she sees him smirk.

"I can not make you believe anything you are not ready to see. When you are ready, you will see and understand, just as she will see the strength inside of you. Now fix your stance."

"The prophecy. How do you know it's right?" she continues, trying to avoid another round of training.

"It is a dream. One that each sage has. When someone replicates the dream, it signals that the current sage will transition to the after realm. Tabatha, I have told you this for days now."

"I have another question."

"You are full of questions today," he grumbles, but waves his hand for her to continue.

"Of all the people, why choose me?"

"Tabatha, I am not the keeper of fate, only the follower. Perhaps one day you will be wise and figure out why you are the Chosen One. Until then, strike."

"But I'm no one. Nothing. I can't keep those I love safe or my mother's diner from falling into ruin."

"Maybe that is not your fate to solve."

Tabatha tilts her head and places her hands on her hips. Eli drops his hands. Sinking to the ground, he calls her over.

"You are as stubborn as my beloved. Tell me what is on your mind so we may train. We have days until the portal reopens, and I want you battle ready."

Feeling nauseous at the reminder, Tabatha graciously sits on the dusty factory floor, ignoring the mice that once sent fear through her.

"I am the Chosen One. Shouldn't I be able to save everything I love?"

He laughs, "Fate is a cruel mystery that rarely allows us to have what we truly want."

"That's a terrible answer," she says.

Eli smiles and shrugs his shoulders, "Tabatha, no one said being the Chosen One was glamorous. There is always a price to pay."

"Well, I want it all," she pouts.

"And what does it all look like, Tabatha?"

She opens her mouth, but stops, unsure what she desires. She has always been told what to have, who to be, and where to go.

"What do I want?" she murmurs.

Eli stands and dusts the dirt from his pants, "We are done today."

"What? Why?" she questions.

"A better assignment will be for you to figure out what you want."

"But don't I have to help you? Let's train. I'm ready."

Fear pushes her after him, as her heart tells her she is not ready to let him go.

"Eli, I'm ready. Don't go," her voice cracks, sending chills through her.

The big man sighs but does not turn to her, "Tabatha, I need you. I can not return home without the Chosen One. But you must choose this. You must make a decision you stand behind. I can not do that for you. Take this time and get your affairs in order. If you choose the path that fate has ordained for you, I will see you at the destination on the new Leo Moon. If you are not there, we go our separate paths."

"But then you won't see your family."

"No, I won't. And all my people will perish. But I will have to accept what fate has in store for me. Goodbye, Tabatha."

Leaving her, she hangs on every footfall as the last echo of his steps dwindles away, leaving Tabatha with questions only she can answer.

"Am I afraid of fate? Of choosing me?" she whispers.

Her voice carries, but no answers travel back.

For the first time, sitting on the cold dusty floor of an abandoned factory, Tabatha is alone. Truly alone. She has no one to turn to for advice. No one ordering her to make a choice. Yet, she longs for direction. Afraid her choice will be wrong, she sits staring where Eli once was.

She runs her fingers through her curls, and huffs, "This is what I get for saying I want to lead."

CHAPTER FORTY-SIX

46

Tabatha feels as lonely as the grey wispy clouds drifting in front of the sun. They are a sliver of something that once was fluffy and bright. She, like the clouds, is a mix of something that is barely present.

Tabatha has felt increasingly lonely in the days she has been without Eli. She wakes, hoping to see him laid on the couch or perched in the corner as his eyes watch the door. But sadly, each morning brings with it the realization that he is gone. Tabatha follows their routine, up at dawn, and training until the sun is too hot to bear. She hopes following their regimen will bring her back to him, but true to his words; he has allowed her space to think. But thinking is far from what she can do, she only worries.

Tabatha worries about Sam's promise to remove her brother and every reminder of her mother from the diner. She fears confronting her brother and being vulnerable about her true feelings. She shudders at the thought of losing Eli forever, or worse, that his words about a portal and a prophecy are real.

Drawing her knees close to her body, Tabatha hugs herself close. Amongst all the questions is one sure thing, tonight everything will change. The day of Sam's ultimatum and the destined portal date are here. Today, she can not delay any further; she must face her fears. Tabatha must disappoint someone, but will that person be herself?

Turning toward the alley, she sees Daniel unlock the diner's side door. Knowing what must be done does not make the task any easier. Even as she leaves the apartment, she does not know what she will say to Daniel. She has no idea if he will understand her emotions or if he will look at her with the same anger as their last encounter.

Reaching the heavy metal door, her hand trembles. A door she once swung open with ease now seems too daunting to touch.

She looks up at the apartment, and sadness squeezes her heart. Eli is not there to guide her through what she must do, nor is his presence a reminder that she has someone to rely on if her brother rejects her.

She places a hand on the door and breathes through the shakiness in her body. She won't run, she tells herself as she pulls the spare key from her pocket.

The lock turns, and the door swings open. The once familiar walls feel empty of her mother's joy.

"Hello?" she calls out, as she hears the creak of Daniel's chair. She calls out, not wanting to surprise him, as she usually does upon her arrival. She knows where he will be, huddled in his office, reviewing the books and trying to remedy any mishaps. But with her absence, would there be any mistakes to fix?

Before she reaches the end of the hall, Daniel is there. She takes a step back, unsure of his expression. She sees a strain on his face, which is more than she has experienced before. Tabatha takes another step back, preparing to leave when his face softens.

"Tabatha," he says, wrapping her in an embrace.

His touch feels as it did when they were children. Full of love and protection. Her arms wrap around him, and the apprehension she has fades.

Their embrace lasts long, and she questions why she even doubted his affection for her.

Daniel pulls away and looks her over, inspecting her as if she is as fragile as glass.

"I'm okay," she laughs, twirling for him to see how whole she is.

His eyes glisten, and her heart aches for the pain she has caused him.

"Tabatha, when Sam came here looking for you, I was so worried. I did not know you weren't with him. Where were you?"

It takes a moment for Tabatha to clear the ache in her chest. Clearing her throat, she speaks, "I was upstairs in the apartment. I didn't want you to see me, so I tried to sneak around when you wouldn't be here."

She chooses her words carefully, avoiding any mention of Eli. She doesn't want Daniel to worry or to see her actions as reckless, not after he has been worried about her safety.

"I had so much on my mind, I didn't think to look there. Tabatha, I should have never told you to leave," he says, pacing back into the kitchen.

She follows him, joy filling her heart. Her anger toward him flees, as she remembers being by his side. If he regrets his words, what else does he wish to take back?

"Daniel, it's okay. It doesn't matter."

"Are you hungry?" he asks, removing plates from the fridge.

She smiles, knowing he can hardly boil an egg, "Daniel, I am fine. I'm a big girl. I promise."

She pushes him to the side, putting back the eggs and cases of bread. She opts for a slice of cake and takes a piece for the both of them.

Her heart swells with joy, remembering the late nights spent cleaning and eating by each other's side. Partners. Siblings. Never feeling alone. When did all that change? She ponders.

Nothing matters, not the prophecy, not Sam's words. The only thing of substance is that she has her brother's back. But that all fades when his face turns questioning.

There is the familiar tug of irritation that she can sense from his raised brow. When he speaks, the softness fades, replaced by the subtle hint of irritation, "Why didn't Sam know where you were?"

She doesn't want to disappoint him, but she knows the words she must say. It was unclear before, but a voice rings inside, telling her she can't go back.

Placing the fork on her plate, she says, "I left. I just walked away."

"Why would you leave Sam?"

It is the perplexity in his tone that hurts her the most. It is the faded concern and present judgment that wounds her.

"Sam doesn't make me happy. I know I should go back, but I can't. I want us to work together so we can make Mom's place home again."

Her words do not shift his irritation, "Tabatha, what did you do?"

Daniel backs away from her. His hands run over his face. She watches as he tries to quell his anger, and she can see it clearly. He wasn't afraid for her.

"You weren't worried because I was missing. You're worried because you thought I messed things up with Sam," the words leave her like a whisper and resound in her ear like the drop of a bomb.

He turns to her with a vengeful anger in his eyes. A glare that would have made her quiver, but now makes her ache with disappointment.

"Tabatha, grow up!" he shouts. His voice rattles the hanging ladles and pans. "One day, I'll be gone, and I won't leave you unprotected like Mom did to me. I know he is not the best, but he will provide for you. He's willing to help this place. The last piece of mom we have left. Why would you mess that up?"

She can not find the anger she once had. Can't muster the admiration she once felt. The only thing Tabatha feels is a deep shame and embarrassment.

"I thought you were so much stronger than me. You problem solved and told me you would manage everything. I thought that was because you had the best parts of mom. But you ruined everything she had because you were afraid. All because you didn't trust me."

There are no tears that she can cry to convey the depth of her sorrow, seeing her brother fearful.

"All this time, your anger was a mask for how afraid you are, not because I mess up or cause trouble. It was about you."

"Tabatha, I—"

"I'm not finished," she says, continuing before he tries to speak over her. "Sam told me everything. He told me about how you have already sold the restaurant. I know that he's only entertaining marriage as a courtesy. How could you lie to me?"

"Tabatha, look around. We are struggling. Each day, another place is run out of business and bought out by a face that doesn't look like ours. This keeps mom's place here and keeps us safe."

As she stares at Daniel, frantic and desperate, she is filled with pity. Clutching her fists, she feels the pain of her nails digging into her. The feeling keeps her tears back. Tears she does not want Daniel to see, not because they convey her weakness, but because he won't understand that they show her sadness for his pain.

"All you see is that little girl who still wants her mother back. Daniel, I am weak and, sometimes, even foolish, but I am strong too, stronger than you will ever see, and that makes me sad."

"Tabatha, you are more than your screw-ups. But your actions have real consequences. I'm trying to save you from your reckless actions."

She sighs, knowing they will come to no common ground, "I know every decision you have made was with the best intention for the restaurant and me. But if you had asked me, seen me for who I am, maybe things would have been different."

She looks into his eyes for understanding as she gathers her next words. His hard expression remains, but she does not hold back her words, "I can not marry Sam. I don't know how, but I will get back every last dime he gave you. We won't lose mom's restaurant."

"No," the word is seething with his anger. Anger that causes her to step back. His lips twist into a snarl as he continues, "I'm done protecting you."

"I told you, I would figure out how to get Sam his money. I won't burden you with that."

"You and I both know you can't."

Daniel turns his back on her.

"I know you think I can't figure this out, but I can."

"You can't," his words are dry. His eyes are empty of emotion as he hides behind a stack of papers. He looks at her with all the emotion he has left within him. His words are strained, as if looking at her causes him pain. "I'm done, Tabatha. I can't protect you and fight for this place anymore. I don't want to."

"What does that mean?"

The ticking of the clock fills the silence as Tabatha and her brother do not move. The crumbled edges of the paper show the anger Daniel suppresses.

"It means I won't provide for you anymore. Marry Sam or don't. Either way, I can't deal with your dreams and fairytales anymore. I don't want anything to do with you. The restaurant is mine. Mom left it to me, not you, not our father who left. Do whatever you want, but I will make sure mom's legacy continues."

Daniel ignores Tabatha standing in the doorway, mouth gaping open at his words. He resumes his task shuffling papers and scribbling notes, unfazed by the crushing weight he has placed on his sister.

She aches to undo what has been broken. But the moment ticks on as the sound of servers and chefs enter the kitchen.

Daniel looks up from his task in a manner that causes her to flinch. Tabatha turns to leave before he commands her away, a heartache she fears she cannot take. But she can not leave before he breaks her even further, "You are no longer welcome in the kitchen apartment. I will have the locks changed today."

CHAPTER FORTY-SEVEN

47

Tabatha seethes with anger, so much that even her own power terrifies her. Eli has told her about the alignment of the moon and how its shift will boost her power. But this is from a man who speaks of fairytales. She tells herself, it's not power that flows through her veins, making her body burn like fire; it's rage from her previous encounter.

Her brother wants nothing to do with her. She knows his words will change when she promises to marry Sam. She will make everything okay, even if that means she must walk away from Eli.

She tells herself she can walk that path, tell Sam she will be his bride, and keep her strength burning inside; she must. Tabatha will not leave her brother broken and disheartened, as she saw in his eyes. She will prove to him she is strong. She will save everyone. Isn't that why she's the Chosen One?

Eli will be fine without her. He has proven that to her. She has saved him from the depths of darkness. Tabatha promises she will ensure he makes it to his family, even though she is sure he will leave when he realizes the portal is only in his mind.

There are no more tears within her, only the electric sensation coursing through Tabatha as she marches forward. The stench of the putrid river flowing beside the underpass almost makes her turn away. But she is not ready to go back to Sam's home. Not ready to tell him he's won. She will strike up her own deal, she tells herself. But something in her whispers she's not going back.

Tabatha inches closer to stairs that lead to some unknown place, yet something within her tells her she is in the meeting place of the new moon and city center. The place where alignment and new beginnings are most strong. But if this is the beginning, why does she feel like so much is ending?

Her steps slow when she sees a dark figure approaching from the stairs. When the man comes into focus, she is filled with renewed sadness.

"Eli," she says, but finds she can say no more. The thought of this being their goodbye pains her to silence as the big man approaches with a vigor and intensity that makes his steps barely touch the ground.

He laughs, "I told you, you would feel fate pulling you if you listened to the flow of the land."

His joy is effervescent. It touches Tabatha, making her smile, even though it fails to reach her heart.

Eli reaches her and spins Tabatha around. Eli dances her around to music only he can hear. His playfulness sparks laughter from her, even though the joy does not touch her soul.

Thinking of how she may hurt him, she pulls away.

"So this is it?" the words almost refuse to come out.

"This is it," he says, his confidence overshadowing the questioning of her tone.

"Remind me again how you know the portal will open tonight?" Tabatha stalls, trying to gather her words for goodbye.

"We are entering a new moon in Leo. This is a season of new beginnings. Tonight is the beginning when the moon and sun will align with the elements of my world. At precisely the right time, I will have access to my abilities and the moon's strength, which will allow me to open the portal. We will have to wait another year to enter the season if we miss this opportunity. By then, it could be too late. Even now, I do not know what fate has befallen my people."

There is an air of concern in his voice as he draws her down to the underpass.

"You're confident this will work?" she asks.

Eli doesn't hear the surprise in her voice, and if he does, his words do not show it, "I am confident because I found you. When I was in a place of deep despair, as the prophecy foretold, I found hope. Thoughts of failing consumed me, and fear of never returning home to my loved ones sent me into a darkness blacker than the darkest night. But then I saw you. That changed everything."

Eli grasps her arm and squeezes it gently. Tabatha pulls away for fear he will feel how she shakes.

Turning away from him, she places her hands to her mouth, both to quell the scream rising inside and to stop her words from leaving her lips. Her heart pounds as she feels as small as the mice scurrying in the distance.

The clouds part, revealing the pale silvery glow of the new moon. As if tied to the moon, the burning looming inside Tabatha ignites until she can no longer take it.

"Eli, I have something to say. I—"

"Do you feel that? It's time. Our window will be small. Any form of hesitation could cost us this moment."

He looks at her with a light as brilliant as a thousand burning stars, and for a moment, she hopes his words are true. She clings to the promise that he will open a portal and see his family on the other side. While her mind tells her it is all a fantasy, if it means he gets to hold on to his light, she desires it more than anything.

She nods, forgetting about her words of goodbye and ultimatums that seek to take her joy.

Eli turns from her, and he outstretches his arms. It's a grand gesture, and for a moment, nothing happens. Then the wind flows, kicking dust around their feet.

A chesty laugh rumbles from Eli, "It has been so long since I felt this flow of energy."

He shifts his body as his arms and hands pull at the air. Tabatha watches as the wind whips faster, chilling her cheeks. The wind skips faster, pulling her curls from her tie.

Tabatha watches in unbelief as the air before her sparks. "This can't be happening," she breathes, feeling the ground quake and the electric flow of energy pulsing in the air.

"I can feel it. We're almost there," he calls over the sound of whirling wind and crackling lightning.

Tabatha's heart pounds wildly as Eli's movements manipulate the electric sparks into a portal. Her eyes frantically look beyond him to a world with vibrant green hills and an ocean so blue it would envy the sky.

He calls to Tabatha, drawing her focus back to this world, "The new moon is in position, and the portal will close in 3 minutes and 47 seconds."

Eli extends his large hand to her, beckoning for her to follow.

Her knees quiver, telling her to flee. The unreal is before her eyes as she recounts their time together. The crazed man filled with dissolution was true to his word. On the day and hour that he predicted, everything he said has come to pass. Yet everything in her being screams he is wrong about her.

Her head shakes as she struggles to find her words. Her mind tells her to breathe and her body to run.

"Eli, I can't, and I won't," Tabatha shouts over the windstorm caused by his portal.

Tabatha pivots, running from Eli and what could be her destiny.

Meet the author

Liz Bullard is a passionate author and podcast host, whose love of reading has propelled her into the world of writing. Committed to creating vibrant communities, she can be found planting seedlings in local gardens or connecting with other authors on her popular eReads Podcast. When she's not working hard, Liz enjoys cooking with her corgi Preston by her side and curling up with a good book. With a flair for storytelling and an enthusiasm for learning, Liz is always looking forward to her next creative endeavor. In addition to being a self-published author, Liz is also signed to Tabletop Publishing and will have her first children's book coming out in 2025.

Want more Liz Bullard? See what's coming next, win advance copies, and find deals.

The official Liz Bullard newsletter

www.LizBullardWrites.com

f facebook.com/eReadsPodcast

instagram.com/lizbullardwrites/

http://pinterest.com/lizbullardwrites/

tiktok.com/@lizbullardwrites

https://twitter.com/ereadspodcast

youtube.com/channel/UCTd6bsxiSdmH0X43EuYPQcQ

Follow the series

Snow Fall: A Prophecy Series Short Christmas Story

Join Tabatha, the Chosen One, as she embarks on a winter wonderland journey full of surprises! With her elemental powers and a little bit of charm, she'll bring cheer to the warriors of Zodia and prove that sometimes joy comes with disaster. Celebrate the season with this magical holiday tale of adventure, secrets, and good old-fashioned festive fun!

The Prophecy Series, a three-part adventure, is set in a fantastical world rife with elemental magic and mighty warriors.

This novella, a short side adventure, introduces the world of Zodia and the central characters.

Prophecy Trilogy: New Moon

In "New Moon," the battle between fate and the unseen unfolds in a land of elemental magic, where disobedience can lead to death. Eli is sent on an impossible mission to seek out the Chosen One, Tabatha, a task that no one has ever returned from. His loyalty and obedience are put to the test as he faces a darkness that only the Chosen One can defeat.

As Tabatha is thrust into the spotlight as the Chosen One, she must navigate her newfound power and the weight of destiny on her shoulders. With the fate of the land hanging in the balance, will she answer the call and rise to the challenge, or will she succumb to the shadows?

Prophecy Trilogy: Portal

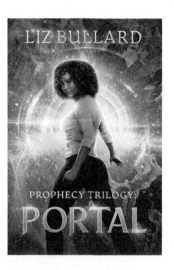

Step into a world of enchantment and suspense in "Portal," the electrifying second installment of the Prophecy Trilogy. Tabatha, the Chosen One, embarks on a captivating journey of self-discovery that weaves a web of betrayal and unexpected twists. Prepare to be captivated as her struggle to master her powers sets off a chain of events that threatens to shatter her newfound family and test her resilience.

But the story doesn't end there. Eli and Talia, each battling their own inner demons, strive to reunite after years of separation. Will they find solace in each other's arms, or will the forces that tore them apart be too powerful to overcome?

Made in the USA
Middletown, DE
09 September 2024

60072205R00126